SCOOBY-DOO! STORYBOOK COLLECTION

WB WORLDWIDE PUBLISHING ™

SCHOLASTIC INC.

New York   Toronto   London   Auckland   Sydney
Mexico City   New Delhi   Hong Kong   Buenos Aires

ISBN 0-439-51320-0
Compilation copyright © 2002 by Hanna-Barbera.
Scooby-Doo in Jungle Jeopardy copyright © 2001 by Hanna-Barbera.
Scooby-Doo and the Opera Ogre copyright © 2001 by Hanna-Barbera.
Scooby-Doo and the Alien Invaders copyright © 2000 by Hanna-Barbera.
Scooby-Doo and the Weird Water Park copyright © 2000 by Hanna-Barbera.
Scooby-Doo and the Phantom Cowboy copyright © 2002 by Hanna-Barbera.
Scooby-Doo and the Witch's Ghost copyright © 1999 by Hanna-Barbera.
Scooby-Doo and the Fantastic Puppet Factory
copyright © 2000 by Hanna-Barbera.
Scooby-Doo and the Marsh Monster copyright © 2002 by Hanna-Barbera.
SCOOBY-DOO and all related characters and elements are trademarks of and © Hanna-Barbera.
(s02)

Designed by Louise Bova
12 11 10 9 8 7 6 5 4 3 2 1   2 3 4 5 6/0
All text by Jesse Leon McCann, except *Scooby-Doo and the Witch's Ghost*,
by Gail Herman
Special thanks to Duendes del Sur for interior illustrations.
Printed in Singapore   46
First printing, November 2002

CONTENTS

SCOOBY-DOO! in JUNGLE JEOPARDY™

by Jesse Leon McCann

For my mother, Mary Weidner, who kept a roof
over my head and protected me.
And for Bill Weidner, who now protects her.

Scooby-Doo and his pals from Mystery, Inc. were visiting Central America. One of Daphne's teachers, Professor Peabody, was an expert in archaeology, the science of uncovering ancient objects buried a long time ago. He was involved with a lot of other scientists in a dig deep in the jungle, and he had invited the kids to join him.

"Daphne!" Professor Peabody greeted them warmly. "I'm so glad you and your friends are here! The expedition is about to begin."

"What are we looking for, professor?" Daphne asked as they ventured into the lush jungle.

"I've heard legends from the local natives about an undiscovered Mayan pyramid around here," the professor explained. "The other scientists think I'm an old fool on a wild goose chase."

"Like, professor, I don't see a pyramid, but there's some sort of old *blocky* place over there!" Shaggy pointed to a spot through trees and vines. An ancient building was barely visible.

The professor was overjoyed. "My dear boy, that *is* a pyramid! A Mayan pyramid! You found it!"

Their happy mood was soon cut short, however. The pyramid had a guardian — a fierce, catlike creature that came out snarling at them! And as it snarled, a volcano erupted!

Scooby-Doo was ready to attack the creature. He didn't like mean cats, no matter how big they were!

"Scooby, this is the *first* time we've had to convince you to run away," Fred said. "But we'd better retreat and think about this!"

They ran, with the snarling cat creature following right behind. Luckily, about a quarter mile from the scientists' camp, the creature stopped chasing them.

When Professor Peabody and the gang told the other scientists what they'd seen, they all laughed.

"It figures you'd find some kids to believe your crackpot theories," said a scientist named McGurty.

"I'm a laughingstock!" Professor Peabody said. "I need to bring back proof, not wild tales. I'm getting too old for this."

"Nonsense," Daphne replied. "You just need a little help."

"That's right," agreed Fred. "Let us figure out the mystery behind this cat creature, then you can get back to work."

Soon the gang was back where they'd seen the creature. They passed some spooky-looking idols. Scooby did not like them one bit!

"Let me get this straight — you're not afraid of six-foot cats, but these hunks of rock creep you out?" Velma asked, smiling.

"Reah," replied Scooby. "Rou ret!"

Scooby was so scared, he wouldn't go a step further. But Velma had an idea.

"Wow, look at all the fresh fruit on the trees!" she said. "Sure looks yummy!"

"You know, Scoob, Velma's right." Shaggy smacked his lips. "Like, those goodies look ripe for the picking!"

"Reah, reah!" Scooby licked his own lips.

Scooby and Shaggy filled their arms with all kinds of fruit. Soon they couldn't see where they were going!

"Look out!" cried the others. But it was too late!

15

"Zoinks!"

Down they fell! They hit the bottom of the pit with a thud. Luckily it wasn't *that* far down — their backsides just got a little sore.

The rest of the gang ran to the hole and looked down.

"Stay there!" shouted Fred. "We'll throw you down a light!"

Soon Shaggy and Scooby had a torch rigged up. It was a great relief that they didn't have to find their way out in the dark.

But Shaggy was still nervous. "Like, Scoob, I get the funny feeling we're being watched!"

Scooby gulped. Shaggy quickly lit the torch.

Suddenly, they were surrounded by bats! *Vampire* bats! The torch light had startled the sleeping creatures and sent them swarming through the cave. When the bats saw the yummy fruit on the ground, they just had to bite into it.

The sight of the bats' sharp teeth biting into the fruit sent Shaggy and Scooby into a panic.

"Zoinks!" cried Shaggy. "Like, let's get out of here *fast*, before we're next on the menu!"

Scooby nodded. "Real rast!"

They ran deeper into the cave, getting more and more lost.

"Shaggy! Scooby! Don't run away!" Velma called. "The bats won't hurt you!"

"It's too late. They're gone!" Fred said. "Let's climb down after them."

But before they could, Velma made an interesting discovery. "Hey, this cave entrance looks like it leads down to the same place!" she said to the others. "Let's go!"

"I'd like it a lot more if the cave didn't look like a cat," Daphne said, shuddering.

Little did they know they were being watched by a pair of eyes. *Cat's* eyes!

Unaware they were being watched, the three friends headed for the cave entrance. Without warning, there came a rumbling sound!

Daphne, Velma, and Fred looked up. An avalanche of heavy tree trunks was rolling their way! They had no choice but to run as fast as they could, staying just in front of the runaway logs.

"Jeepers, that was a trap!" Daphne yelled above the noise. "Somebody cut those logs loose just when we got near!"

"Not only that, we're coming to a big river!" Velma pointed ahead. "What'll we do?"

"The only thing we *can* do," Fred shouted. "Jump!"

They jumped into the swiftly moving river and were carried away by the strong current.

Splash! The logs rolled into the river behind them.

"Jinkies! Grab hold of a log and hang on!" Velma cried.

They quickly climbed aboard a sturdy trunk and looked around. That made them feel better — for a minute. Then they heard it.

There was a roaring waterfall up ahead!

The three kids didn't have a chance to escape the waterfall. Over they went! They plunged down, down, down! It was more than a hundred feet to the bottom!

Luckily, there was a deep pool at the bottom of the falls. Soon Fred, Daphne, and Velma had swam back up to the surface.

"Boy, that was one lucky break." Fred started swimming ashore. "Come on, let's find Shaggy and Scooby."

But as they swam to the shore, they suddenly didn't feel very lucky at all. Standing there were *three* cat creatures!

Meanwhile, Shaggy and Scooby were deep underground, trying to find their way out. The torch helped a lot, but they could only see a few feet in front of them.

As they crept along, Shaggy kept hearing a funny hissing noise. "Like, say, Scoob, do you hear that?" Shaggy asked. "It sounds like someone left the gas on."

Scooby listened. Then he gulped. "Raggy! Rot ras!" Scooby cried. "Rakes!"

Shaggy laughed. "Like, don't be silly, Scoob. Rakes don't hiss!"

Then Shaggy held the torch up higher. Right in front of them were hundreds of squirming, crawly creatures.

"Zoinks!" Shaggy yelled. "You meant snakes!"

Scooby and Shaggy knew they had to get away from the snakes as fast as possible. Unfortunately, they were surrounded!

"Like, now what?" Shaggy said. "We're going to end up a snake snack!"

Just then, Scooby noticed some steps carved into the stone wall behind them. He pulled Shaggy up the stairs and away from the snakes. They were safe!

But now they had another problem. Their torch was sputtering and looked like it was going to go out. Not only that, they both thought they saw a chamber up ahead . . . guarded by some strange creatures!

Finally, their torch went out. At first Shaggy and Scooby were terrified. Then they realized they could still see! Light was coming from the chamber ahead.

They quietly sneaked up to the chamber's entrance. *Whew!* The shadows they'd seen weren't creatures after all, just more stone idols.

When they looked around, their mouths dropped wide open. The entire chamber was an ancient Mayan temple!

Scooby was just about to whoop with relief! But Shaggy quickly put his hand over Scooby's mouth.

"Like, quiet, Scoob!" Shaggy warned in a whisper. "Somebody lives here. Who do you think lit those torches?"

"Roh, right." Scooby was suddenly wide-eyed. "Rorry, Raggy."

"Like, let's take a look around — *quietly*!" Shaggy replied.

Shaggy and Scooby didn't have much of a chance to explore the chamber. Behind them, they heard the sound of footsteps approaching. The two friends quickly hid behind one of the huge idols.

They couldn't believe their eyes when they saw who'd entered!

"Zoinks!" whispered Shaggy. "It's those cat creeps! And they've got Fred and the girls!"

"*Grrrrrr*," Scooby growled. He really didn't like cats — or creepy cat creatures. And now they had his friends!

"Like, it's nice you want to save our friends, Scoob," Shaggy said, holding Scooby back. "But let's wait for a better chance — like maybe when we have an *army* with us!"

But Scooby pulled and pulled. Shaggy held tight onto his collar, and pushed on the stone idol for support. Without meaning to, Shaggy pushed the statue over.

Smash! The cats whirled at the noise.

"Oh . . . l-like, hi," Shaggy stammered. "We're from animal control. Just making sure your kitty licenses are up-to-date!"

The cats snarled and jumped toward them.

"Zoinks! Run, Scoob, before we become their new scratching posts!"

Scooby suddenly realized he was no match for the scary cat creatures. He ran. But while the cats went after him and Shaggy, Fred, Velma, and Daphne escaped!

The three friends cut their bindings away on a sharp rock. Then they went searching for Scooby and Shaggy.

They found them hiding in a cave with crystal in the walls. There were finely grained crystals under their feet, too. Velma reached down and grabbed a handful. She tasted it.

"Just as I thought. We're in an underground salt mine!"

"Like, you ever get the sinking feeling you were . . . sinking?" Shaggy gulped.

It was true. The kids were sinking in the salt! And when the cats found them, it didn't matter. The gang couldn't run because they were stuck in the salt. It was like quicksand!

But the kids had another stroke of luck: Just after their heads went under, they slid a few feet and landed in a big pile of salt.

"Jinkies!" said Velma happily. "There was a hole at the bottom of the salt pit!"

"Come on, gang," Fred said, starting to walk away. "We don't have much time to spare! Let's get out of here."

They all followed Fred through a nearby tunnel. Before long, they found themselves in a gigantic, round chamber with a hole at the top.

"I think we're in the middle of the volcano!" Fred exclaimed. "And it's hollow!"

"Why would this equipment be here if only the cat creatures live in the caves?" Daphne wondered.

"That's a good question, Daphne," Fred answered. "And that's just what we're going to find out. Let's look around!"

They started investigating the equipment, looking for clues. They hadn't gone very far when, unexpectedly, there came a deep rumbling sound.

Scooby looked up. "Rikes! Rit's a ronster!"

"A monster?" said Velma. "Don't be silly — there's no such thing as monsters!"

"Zoinks! Then there's 'no such thing' after us right now!" cried Shaggy. "Get in the cart and let's get out of here!"

Their cart gained speed as it went deeper underground. If they weren't being chased, it would have been fun — like a roller coaster!

Velma turned to look behind. "That's no monster! It's some sort of machine . . . a steam shovel!"

"Jeepers! And there's a cat creature driving it!" Daphne added.

Luckily, the steam shovel couldn't go very fast. Soon the gang's cart had left it far behind.

"Like, now I'm really confused!" Shaggy said. "Six-foot cats who walk on two legs is one thing, but cats who drive . . . that's kooky!"

Fred pointed. "Uh-oh, I think we're coming to the end of this ride . . . fast!"

Bam! The cart hit the end of the tracks and the gang was spilled into a huge cavern.

When they got up and shook off their dizziness, they were nothing less than amazed!

"Jinkies!" said Velma.

"Jeepers!" said Daphne.

"Zoinks!" said Shaggy.

Scooby just fainted.

"Now I'm starting to get an idea of what's been going on around here!" Fred exclaimed.

Gold! Silver! Diamonds and rubies! The cavern was filled with treasure fit for a King!

"Come on, gang. Those cats will be right behind us," Fred said. "Let's find a way out of here!"

"But, like, aren't we going to do something about this treasure?" asked Shaggy.

"That's *exactly* what we're going to do," Fred answered, "as soon as we're back up to ground level."

Velma was looking in a different tunnel than the one they'd come through. "This passage looks like it goes all the way up! Wake up, Scooby, and let's get going!"

When they got back up to the surface, Fred explained his plan. As they listened, Scooby and Shaggy became very unhappy.

"Like, no way, Fred!" Shaggy shook his head. "Scoob and I aren't going anywhere near those cats. Like, it's in our contracts . . . it's called the *claws* clause!"

"Right!" agreed Scooby.

"Would you do it for some Scooby Snacks?" Velma smiled, waving the tempting treats in front of them.

As usual, Shaggy's and Scooby's stomachs won out over their heads. They soon agreed to do as Fred asked.

Later, at the mouth of the cave, the cat creatures came looking for the kids who had invaded their secret caverns. The cats were shocked when they saw what walked out of the jungle and right up to them.

"Like, howdy!" a cat that looked like Shaggy said. "We're new in the neighborhood, and we were wondering if we could borrow a cup of catnip!"

"Reah!" agreed the cat that looked kind of like a dog.

Velma and Daphne had decorated Shaggy and Scooby to look like cats. They used vines and palm fronds for the costumes.

The cat creatures snarled and chased Shaggy and Scooby. The creatures were so distracted by the crazy cat costumes, they didn't notice what the other kids were doing.

As soon as Shaggy and Scooby led the cats away, Fred pulled on a vine. Several logs the gang had collected came rolling down a hill — right at the cats! Now it was *their* turn to dodge the runaway tree trunks!

The cats snarled and hissed as they tried to avoid the logs. But soon they got away and started chasing Shaggy and Scooby again.

Now Velma went into action. As soon as the cat creatures were under the tree she was hiding behind, Velma pulled on another vine.

Dozens of coconuts came pouring out of the tree! The kids had made a net and filled them with the coconuts. Now they were raining down on the cats and hitting them — hard!

"Like, that's using the old nut, Velma!" Shaggy cheered.

"Reah! Reah!" agreed Scooby happily.

The cats were snarling more than ever. They ran under the tree right next to Velma, Shaggy, and Scooby.

Velma pulled another vine. Another net opened, raining more coconuts on the confused creatures.

The cat creatures were in a panic now. They ran to a clearing where there were no trees, down by the river. When they were close enough, Daphne pulled on a vine that was like a tripwire.

Sploosh! Sploosh!

The cat creatures tripped and went flying into the cold water!

"Help! I can't swim!" yelled one of the creatures.

"Me, neither!" cried another.

"Like, I knew cats hated water, but I've never heard them call for help before!" Shaggy laughed.

"Ree-hee-hee-hee!" Scooby joined in.

The gang pulled the wet cats out of the water and tied them up. Unmasked, they turned out to be McGurty and some other scientists.

"Let me guess," said Velma. "You discovered the hidden treasure and decided to keep it for yourselves."

"You came up with the cat-creature disguise to frighten away anyone who came snooping around," added Daphne.

"And you used explosives to give the illusion that the volcano was active, so no one would think of looking underground," Fred concluded.

McGurty sneered. "It would've worked, too, if it weren't for you meddling kids and that dog of yours!"

Later, after they'd handed the "cats" over to the authorities, the kids showed Professor Peabody where the Mayan temple was. Then they led him down to the treasure cavern.

"Thanks so much, kids, " said the professor. "I am forever in your debt! Think of all the archaeological research in store for us!"

"Like, I'd rather think of all the Scooby Snacks *we* have in store for *us*! Right, Scooby?" Shaggy patted his best pal on the head.

"Scooby-Dooby-Doo!" cheered Scooby.

SCOOBY-DOO!
and the OPERA OGRE ™

by Jesse Leon McCann

In loving memory of my aunt, Loretta Kennedy, who
took me to my first musical.

"Awr-rooooool!" howled Scooby-Doo.

"And, like, la-la-la-la Figaro! Figaro! Figaro!" sang Shaggy.

"All right, you two," Daphne scolded them. "Just because we're going to the opera doesn't mean *you* have to sing!"

Sure enough, the Mystery Machine was pulling up to a fancy theater. But it looked like the opera house was on fire!

"Gee, what's going on here?" Velma asked as the gang climbed out of the Mystery Machine.

"Oh, it's terrible!" cried Mr. Samuels, the owner of the opera house. "Our entire production is ruined!"

All around Mr. Samuels, people were running out of the smoking opera house. There were audience members in fancy clothes, musicians in tuxedos, stage technicians all dressed in black, and performers in Viking costumes.

44

Mr. Samuels told Scooby and the gang what had happened. "The audience was enjoying our debut production of *The Viking Voyage* when all of a sudden, a strange creature swung down from the rafters. He was carrying a torch in his hand, and he lit the stage on fire! There was smoke everywhere, and everyone panicked and ran for the exits!"

"Oh, my goodness! Is everyone okay?" asked Velma.

"Yes, I think so," replied Mr. Samuels. "Except for one person — the star of the opera, Paul Noble! He's missing!"

One of the singers, a man named William Bluster, approached Mr. Samuels. "Don't worry, Samuels," Bluster said. "I can play the lead part. I am an expert in all things theatrical!" With a sniff he added, "Paul Noble probably went home. He's such a coward."

Mr. Samuels didn't know what to do. It was all so confusing. Then the firemen came out of the opera house looking puzzled.

There was no fire inside! Just a lot of smoke.

"Mr. Samuels, do you mind if we take a look inside?" Fred asked. "We're pretty good at solving mysteries like this."

Mr. Samuels was glad for the help. So the gang went inside, eager to find the cause of all the trouble. (Actually, Scooby and Shaggy were hoping to find a snack bar.)

No sooner had they entered the grand theater than a creepy shadow appeared onstage.

"*Stay away! Beware!*" the shadow screamed. "Beware the wrath of the opera ogre!"

"Zoinks!" Shaggy cried. He and Scooby were so scared, they jumped into the orchestra pit. Shaggy ended up leaping headfirst into a big tuba.

"Like, help! I'm blind!" Shaggy hollered.

"Stop fooling around, you two," Velma chided.

Then something strange happened. When Scooby looked up at the gang from the orchestra pit, he realized that he was going *down* — and so was the whole pit!

The orchestra pit worked just like a big elevator! Normally it took the orchestra up to the stage level. Now it took Shaggy and Scooby down to a dark place under the stage, where sets and props were kept.

"Like, wow, Scoob! I'll bet most people don't get to see this area," Shaggy said. "Let's look around!"

"Ruh-ruh!" Scooby shook his head. "Rit's roo rooky!"

"Too spooky?" Shaggy exclaimed. "No way, Scoob! Look, there are the dressing rooms. I'll bet the performers get all sorts of goodies, like fruit baskets and boxes of chocolates!"

"Rhocolates?" Scooby changed his mind. "Ret's ro!"

Scooby and Shaggy went into a dressing room with a gold star on the door. It belonged to the show's star, Paul Noble.

"Groovy, Scoob!" exclaimed Shaggy.

Scooby couldn't agree more. He sat at the makeup table and pretended he was a famous stage actor. He laughed at his reflection. "Ree-hee-hee!"

"Like, let's see what's in the closet," Shaggy said. Then he got a big scare!

"*Rrrrrmmmm!*" said the creature inside, reaching for Shaggy.

"Zoinks! It's a mummy!" Shaggy shouted.

50

Meanwhile, Fred, Daphne, and Velma were exploring the stage area. Off to the side of the main stage area was a place the audience couldn't see, called the "wings."

"This is where they keep the set pieces until they're ready to go onstage," Daphne explained. "And see those ropes? Those are used to raise and lower the scenery."

The kids were so busy looking at the scenery, they didn't see the creepy shadow of the opera ogre behind them on the floor — until it was too late!

Ka-boom! There was a fiery explosion, then out jumped the opera ogre!

"So! You have intruded on my domain, despite my warnings," the ogre said, his eyes glittering. "Now you must face my wrath!"

"Jinkies!" Velma exclaimed. "Let's get out of here! Exit stage left!"

Fred, Daphne, and Velma ran as fast as their feet could carry them! But before they got far, the ogre recited an eerie poem:

"Fire burn and cauldron bubble!
Bring forth my Viking warriors, on the double!"

Suddenly, Fred and the girls were surrounded by an army of ghostlike Vikings, all grinning evilly!

The kids tried to get away, but they took a wrong turn.

"Jeepers!" Daphne shuddered. "This brings new meaning to the phrase 'stage fright'!"

"There's something strange about these Vikings," Velma remarked. "And we're going to get to the bottom of it."

Velma sounded brave, but it was hard not to shiver as the eerie Viking army crept closer!

In another part of the theater, the mummy was chasing Shaggy and Scooby. The two friends ran through the theater's green room with the mummy hot on their tail. Every big theater has a green room. It's the area where actors meet with audience members after a performance. Usually it's a very pleasant place to be. But right then, Scooby and Shaggy didn't find it pleasant at all! The mummy was gaining on them!

Luckily, Shaggy and Scooby were able to pull the old "one-two" on the mummy. The growling creature soon found itself sliding down a laundry chute.

"Like, make sure you use plenty of starch!" Shaggy called down the chute after the mummy.

Scooby got a big laugh out of that. Then he caught a glimpse of something exciting out of the corner of his eye!

"Rook, Raggy!" Scooby pointed.

It was the costume room!

Shaggy and Scooby couldn't resist. They had to try on some costumes.

There were costumes of Kings, soldiers, cowboys, princesses, witches, and vampires!

"Like, we sure could have used disguises like these on some of our adventures!" Shaggy said as he dressed up as a fairy-tale princess. "Right, Scoob?"

"Ruh-huh!" Scooby agreed wholeheartedly, prancing around like a Roman general in battle.

Meanwhile, Fred, Daphne, and Velma were realizing something.

"Those Vikings haven't moved any closer," said Velma.

"And the opera ogre has disappeared!" Daphne added.

"Look!" exclaimed Fred. "These Vikings aren't ghosts after all. They're just big puppets."

The opera ogre had fooled the kids into thinking they were surrounded! Now he was off to cause mischief elsewhere in the theater.

"C'mon, guys." Fred was heading offstage. "Let's see if we can't catch up with that tricky fellow!"

The kids soon found themselves in one of the dressing rooms. It was a big, long room where the chorus actors got ready before the show.

Daphne found a picture of the star, Paul Noble. Someone had drawn a funny face on it. "Boy, someone sure can't stand Paul Noble," she commented.

"Look at this. It could be a clue!" Velma exclaimed. She pointed at a container filled with smoke-making fluid used for special effects.

"And I found these long strips of canvas." Fred frowned. "What are these doing in the actors' dressing room?"

BLUSTER — UNDERSTUDY

SMOKE MACHINE FILLID

Upstairs, Shaggy and Scooby had run into a problem — an ogre of a problem!

Right in the middle of their play-acting, the opera ogre leaped into the costume room with a loud laugh.

"Flee now, or feel the wrath of the opera ogre!" he whispered menacingly.

"Zoinks! No need for wrath-ing, today, Mr. Creepy!" Shaggy cried as he and Scooby fled the room. "We're fleeing! We're fleeing!"

Scooby and Shaggy ran out to an area overlooking the stage. They came to a circular staircase used by the stage crew, and up they went. The opera ogre was close behind!

When Shaggy and Scooby got to the top of the staircase, they came to a locked door. It was a dead end!

"Like, only one way to go, Scoob!" Shaggy pointed to a pole that had a scenery backdrop tied to it. "I hope you're good at hand-over-hand crawling."

Scooby gulped as he peered down at the approaching ogre. "Ri ram row!"

Just as the ogre reached the top of the stairs, Shaggy and Scooby jumped onto the scenery pole. They started climbing away.

But the ogre didn't follow. Instead, he grinned and cut the support rope that was holding up the backdrop!

Down, down, down Shaggy and Scooby fell — and fast!

"Good-bye, Scoob, old pal!" Shaggy sniffled. "Like, it looks like *splats*ville for us!"

"Roh-roh-roh!" Scooby cried.

Then, a miraculous thing happened. Scooby-Doo and Shaggy hit the sail of the Viking boat onstage. The silk of the sail acted like a slide. They glided smoothly toward the bottom!

"Now *that's* more like it," cheered Shaggy.

"Reah! Reah!" Scooby nodded happily.

But just when they thought they were going to get away, free and clear . . .

"Rrrrrmmm!"

"Zoinks!" Shaggy exclaimed. "It's that funky mummy at the bottom of the sail! And it's reaching for us, Scoob!"

The mummy did, indeed, seem to be reaching for them. But when they reached the bottom, the mummy didn't grab them. Instead, the two buddies accidentally kicked the mummy and sent it flying!

Shaggy laughed. "How about that?"

Scooby grinned. "Reah, row arout rat?"

Daphne, Fred, and Velma heard the commotion onstage. So they ran back out to see what was happening.

"Look!" Velma pointed. "There's a mummy chasing Shaggy and Scooby!"

"Let's help them!" Fred said.

The kids started toward Shaggy and Scooby. But before they could get very far . . .

Splat! The opera ogre was cutting heavy sandbags loose overhead, trying to hit the gang.

"Jeepers! It's too dangerous!" Daphne cried. "Get back!"

Shaggy and Scooby were having problems of their own. The mummy chased them into the scenery shop behind the stage. This was the place where the sets were designed, built, and painted.

Crash! Shaggy ran into some old paint cans.

Smash! Scooby skidded into a stack of lumber.

They were so busy running into things, they didn't realize that the mummy was as clumsy as they were.

Bash! The mummy hit its head on a post.

Dashing through the falling sandbags, the rest of the gang joined Shaggy and Scooby in the scenery shop.

"Jinkies! What's all the noise in here?" Velma wondered.

"Like, that crazy mummy is trying to grab us and put one of its creepy curses on us!" Shaggy said.

"Reah, reepy rurses!" Scooby nodded.

"Well, I don't think this mummy can do much to you guys right now," Fred said, examining the unconscious mummy. "It's out cold!"

Just then, Velma made an interesting discovery.

"Hey, look!" she exclaimed. "It's not a real torch at all! It's just a prop made from cellophane and wood, with a tiny light and fan inside!"

"And this is a machine that makes artificial fog and smoke," said Fred. "I think I know what's been going on here."

The kids began to realize that everything was not what it seemed onstage. In fact, Shaggy and Scooby found that out the hard way when they bit into some legs of lamb made out of painted foam!

"Well, two can play at that game," Fred said. "Listen, gang. I've got an idea. . . ."

A short time later, Shaggy and Scooby were back onstage. They were pretending to be Romeo and Juliet.

"I sure hope this works," Shaggy said nervously.

"Rhat right rhough ronder rindow reaks?" Scooby said to Shaggy, playing along.

But the ploy worked. For, just then, the opera ogre appeared, swinging down to get them — just like they wanted!

"Defy me, will you?" growled the ogre. "Very well. You can't escape me now!"

"Zoinks! That's our cue, Scoob!" Shaggy yelled. "Like, let's get out of here!"

The opera ogre chased Shaggy and Scooby off the stage and into one of the hallways.

"Relp! Relp!" Scooby cried.

"Like, just keep running, Scoob!" Shaggy huffed. "If we stop, he'll get us!"

"Oh, I'll get you, I will," sneered the ogre. "And your little dog, too!"

Just when it looked like the ogre was going to nab them for sure, Shaggy and Scooby veered suddenly to one side.

Before the ogre could change direction, he smashed through a canvas wall. He didn't notice it because it was painted to look just like the hallway!

Fred was waiting on the other side. When the ogre crashed through, Fred tied him up as neat as you please!

"Like, that's one snazzy special effect!" Shaggy laughed.

"Ruh-huh!" Scooby agreed.

"Now let's see who this opera ogre really is." Fred ripped off the ogre's mask. "It's that actor, William Bluster!"

"And the mummy is the missing star, Paul Noble!" Daphne exclaimed. "He wasn't trying to get us. He was just asking us to help untie him!"

"I'll bet Bluster kidnapped him," Velma added.

"Yeah! And with Paul Noble out of the way, they would've let me play his part!" growled William Bluster. "The plan would've worked, too, if it weren't for you nosy kids and your dog!"

Just then, Mr. Samuels ran in with the police to take Bluster away.

"Thanks for solving the mystery, kids!" Mr. Samuels said. "What can I do to repay you?"

"Well, there *is* one thing." Shaggy smiled at Scooby.

"Reah! Reah!" said Scooby excitedly.

Later, the audience was back in their seats. The opera began with Paul Noble in the lead, just where he belonged. Only now there were two new members in the Viking chorus — Scooby and Shaggy!

"Like, this is the grooviest reward of all!" Shaggy said.

And even in the last row, you could hear Scooby loud and clear when he sang out, "Scooby-Dooby-Doo!"

Based on the screenplay
"*Scooby-Doo and the Alien Invaders*"
by **Davis Doi** and **Lance Falk**

Adapted by **Jesse Leon McCann**
Story by **Davis Doi** and **Glenn Leopold**

Scooby and his pals from Mystery, Inc. were traveling through the desert in the Mystery Machine. But then a big sandstorm struck, and Shaggy had trouble driving.

"Like, I can't see a thing!" cried Shaggy as he accidentally turned down the wrong road.

The sandstorm was so thick, no one noticed a **NO TRESPASSING** sign they passed. Suddenly, the whole van was bathed in a bright light from above!

It looked like a giant spaceship! It whooshed by so fast, it spun the Mystery Machine around and around. Shaggy couldn't keep control, and the van ran into a cactus. *Bamm!*

When Scooby and the gang climbed out, the ship was gone.

"What was that thing?" Velma asked.

"Was it some kind of jet?" wondered Daphne.

"Not like any jet I've ever seen," said Fred. "Did you see how fast it was?"

The van wouldn't start again. Fred suggested they walk to a nearby town for help.

"There's snakes and stuff out there in the desert!" Shaggy gulped.

"Reah! Rattlerakes. Sssssssss!" Scooby hissed. He and Shaggy decided to stay behind and guard the van. But as soon as the others were gone, they immediately started looking for Scooby Snacks. There was only one left!

They both grabbed for it, but it fell, bounced across the ground, and was picked up by a strange animal!

"Zoinks! A jackalope!" Shaggy exclaimed. "I thought those things were fake."

"Ree, roo!" Scooby agreed.

The jackalope hopped off with the Scooby Snack. Shaggy and Scooby ran after it.

"Hey, put that down!" Shaggy shouted.

They chased the jackalope to a nearby hill. It ran into a tunnel that glowed with an eerie golden light. As they peered in, Scooby and Shaggy got the strange feeling they were not alone. They turned around and got a big surprise!

"*Rahhhhh!* Raliens!"

Shaggy and Scooby raced away as fast as they could. Two scary-looking aliens followed right behind on their space cycles.

Shaggy and Scooby tried disguising themselves as a pair of cacti, but that didn't fool the aliens. The two friends ran up and down hills, but they couldn't lose the creepy space critters.

Finally, they knocked loose some big, flat stones and rode them like sleds down the hill. They slid all the way to the nearby town and left their pursuers far behind!

Shaggy and Scooby ran into the town diner. Fred, Daphne, and Velma were inside. Scooby and Shaggy told them all about their alien encounter.

Aliens? The rest of the gang didn't know what to think.

"They're real!" shouted a crazy-looking man named Lester. "Them aliens are here to take over the world!"

"Have you had some contact with aliens?" asked Velma.

"That's right," said Lester. "Took me aboard their ship, they did!"

Lester told them about his close encounter aboard the alien spaceship. Since the gang couldn't get the van to a mechanic until morning, he offered to let them spend the night at his place. Lester had all sorts of kooky alien stuff.

Daphne saw some satellite dishes through Lester's window. "What are those?" she asked.

"S.A.L.F. dishes," Lester explained. "The government put 'em up. S.A.L.F. means Search for Alien Life-forms. Ever since they built them dishes, aliens started showing up."

Lester didn't have a lot of room. Shaggy and Scooby had to sleep on his roof in a couple of lawn chairs, but they didn't mind.

"Hey! It's pretty groovy up here," Shaggy remarked.

"Ruh-huh!" Scooby agreed.

Soon they were fast asleep and snoring under a desert sky full of beautiful, twinkling stars.

But one of the lights twinkling overhead wasn't a star — it was a spaceship! It hovered over them, dropped claws down, and lifted them up inside!

Scooby and Shaggy didn't stir until they were strapped to the aliens' laboratory tables.

"Hey! Let us go!" Shaggy cried. "We taste terrible! Like, I'm all stringy."

Scooby was very scared, even though some of the experiments tickled.

"Do not fear us, earth creatures," said one of the aliens. "Cooperate and you will not be harmed."

But when the aliens weren't looking, Scooby used his tail to push a button that released him. He jumped up and ran away, pushing Shaggy's table as he went.

"Sorry, but our health plans don't cover exams!" Shaggy yelled as Scooby pulled him away. The angry aliens chased them all over the spaceship. Shaggy and Scooby couldn't find a way out. Suddenly, a third alien appeared out of nowhere. *Pow!* They ran right into it!

This alien was much bigger than the other two. It pulled out an evil-looking device with all sorts of snapping blades and held it toward Scooby and Shaggy. They fainted dead away.

When they woke up, Shaggy and Scooby were back in the desert and the aliens were gone. They thought they were alone, but then they heard a voice.

"Hey, man, are you all right?"

The two friends couldn't believe their eyes. Standing in front of them was a pretty teenager named Crystal and her dog, Amber. They were the most beautiful girls Shaggy and Scooby had ever seen! Suddenly, the aliens didn't seem so important. In fact, Scooby and Shaggy thought the whole thing had been a nightmare.

"I'm a freelance photographer," Crystal explained. "I'm shooting some desert wildlife for a magazine."

Shaggy told Crystal about the jackalope and the aliens while Scooby showed off for Amber. Crystal asked Shaggy to show her where they'd seen the aliens and the jackalope.

As they walked toward Crystal's Jeep, Shaggy leaned over to Scooby. "Scoob, ol' buddy, I don't know about you," he whispered, "but I think I just found my dream girl."

"Ree, roo!" Scooby nodded.

After Fred took the Mystery Machine to a repair garage, he and the girls decided to check out the S.A.L.F. satellite dishes. They were given a tour by a big guy named Max and his coworkers, Laura and Steve.

"We're monitoring the cosmos twenty-four hours a day, seven days a week," Max explained.

Steve told them how boring the job was. They rarely heard or saw anything promising. But if there was even a tiny chance of making contact with aliens, it was worth it.

Meanwhile, Shaggy and Scooby showed Crystal and Amber the tunnel where they had followed the jackalope and had first seen the aliens. Suddenly, they were surprised by a gruff voice.

"What are you doing here?" Two military policemen appeared in front of them.

"Just taking some wildlife photos," Crystal told them.

"You aren't supposed to be here," said one of the M.P.s. "This area is under government investigation."

The M.P.s checked Crystal's camera, then made them leave.

After they finished their tour of the satellite station, Fred, Daphne, and Velma decided to check out a place called Scorpion Ridge. Max said the government had sent an investigation team there to look into reports about aliens.

They asked Lester to give them a ride to Scorpion Ridge. On the way there, Velma tried to figure things out. "Did you notice that Max, Laura, and Steve all had mud on their shoes?" she asked. "Where would there be mud around here?"

After the M.P.s had gone, Crystal wanted to go back to the strange tunnel. The boys didn't want to go, but when Crystal insisted, they reluctantly followed her and Amber inside.

It was really spooky inside the tunnel. Crystal guided the way with her flashlight as the tunnel led to a big cavern.

"I think I see something ahead," Crystal said.

"Like, the exit, I hope," gulped Shaggy as Scooby moaned in agreement.

Suddenly, they all stopped and gazed at the cavern walls in amazement.

Gold! The cavern walls were lined with gold!

"Scoob, ol' buddy, we've hit the jackpot!" Shaggy said excitedly. "We can buy our own food court!"

"Reah! Rooby Rhax, roo!" Scooby agreed, his eyes sparkling.

"Scooby Snacks?" Shaggy laughed. "With this much gold, we can buy a Scooby Snacks factory!"

"Reah! Reah!"

But their excitement didn't last long. Just then, two aliens jumped out at them. Once more, Shaggy and Scooby were running from the aliens — and this time Crystal and Amber were, too!

At the same time, Fred, Daphne, and Velma had made a discovery at Scorpion Ridge. They'd found the entrance to the gold mine, too — *and* all sorts of mining equipment. In fact, they were surprised to see two military policemen operating the equipment.

Before they had much time to investigate, they were attacked by aliens. The aliens had lost Shaggy, Scooby, and their new friends, but now they had new victims!

The big alien chased Fred, Daphne, and Velma into a trap. Before they knew it, they were swept up into a net.

"You monsters!" cried Daphne.

"Silence, earthling!" said one of the smaller aliens. "You should not have interfered!"

Velma just smiled. "You can give up the hokey alien charade now . . . Steve."

The surprised alien slowly took off his mask. Sure enough, it was Steve from the satellite station. The alien next to him was Laura, and the big alien was Max.

Steve, Max, and Laura told them how they had discovered the gold mine and how they kept the locals away with the alien story. They built a phony spaceship out of a helicopter and hired a couple of friends to pretend to be military policemen.

"I knew it was all a fake!" said Fred.

"Well, it doesn't help you now," sneered Steve. He pulled a lever and the net swung over a deep, dark pit. Steve was going to drop them in!

The two M.P.s went in search of Shaggy, Scooby, Crystal, and Amber. Soon they found them and chased them to the edge of a cliff that dropped off into a dark abyss.

Shaggy and Scooby turned to face the big men. They started making karate movements to try and frighten the M.P.s. They were very pleased when the M.P.s suddenly looked scared, turned, and ran away.

They didn't realize that Crystal and Amber had transformed themselves. They were *real* aliens!

Shaggy and Scooby chased the M.P.s all the way back to where the others were being held. Crystal and Amber had changed back to their human forms, so Shaggy and Scooby had no idea what had really scared the M.P.s.

"Like, stand aside, ladies," Shaggy said. "This is man's work."

"But, Shaggy . . ." Crystal started to warn him.

Before they knew what happened, Shaggy and Scooby were knocked to the ground by the big M.P.s. It wasn't a total loss — Fred, Daphne, and Velma used the diversion to escape!

Amber and Crystal were angry that their friends were being treated so roughly. So they transformed back into their alien forms. Fred, Daphne, and Velma couldn't believe their eyes.

"Jinkies!" exclaimed Velma.

Amber grabbed a steal girder and, using superhuman strength, twisted it around Max and the two big military policemen. They were trapped tight!

Shaggy and Scooby were just coming to when they glimpsed Amber and Crystal as aliens. They were so frightened they screamed.

Just as Velma was explaining who the aliens were, they heard a loud sound.

Suddenly, Steve appeared on a huge tractor. He was heading straight for Crystal and Amber! Crystal tripped and was about to be run over when Amber grabbed the tractor's shovel and bravely held back the machine.

But Amber wasn't strong enough to hold back the tractor for long. Everyone could tell that she was getting weaker and would soon lose her grip.

That's when Shaggy and Scooby-Doo saved the day! They drove in on another tractor, headed straight for Steve.

Scooby looked like he was a knight from the days of old, charging in with a lance to save his lady love. "Rooby-rooby-roo!" he roared.

Steve tried to back up his tractor and get away. But Shaggy sideswiped him and his tractor tumbled over!

"I don't believe it!" cried Steve, staring at Crystal and Amber.

"Come on, let's get out of here!" Laura yelled as she and Steve ran toward the mine's exit.

Fred jumped over to the control lever that held the net in the air. He flipped the switch and dropped it right on top of Steve and Laura. Now they were trapped, too.

"Yes!" cheered Fred.

Now that the mystery was solved and all the villains were captured, Amber and Crystal transformed back to their human forms.

"We were sent by our world to investigate signals from your planet," Crystal explained.

"Transmitted by the S.A.L.F. station," Amber added, and everyone gasped.

Shaggy looked at Amber. "You can talk?"

"Yes, quite well," Amber replied.

"Dig that, Scoob!" laughed Shaggy. "A talking dog!"

Suddenly there was a loud humming sound. A spaceship appeared above them, hovering over a hole in the cavern roof. It was the same ship the gang had seen during the sandstorm.

"Here's our ride," Crystal said.

"We have to go," Crystal said as she hugged Shaggy good-bye. "I hope you can forgive us for deceiving you."

"Yeah, like, we understand," Shaggy replied.

"You are really a groovy guy, Shaggy." Crystal smiled and gave him a quick kiss.

Amber held Scooby's paws. "Good-bye, Scooby. I'll never forget you."

"Ree, roo, Ramber," Scooby said sadly.

The two aliens stepped into the light under the spaceship, waved one last good-bye, and were instantly gone.

Soon the FBI and the police had arrived to take the villains into custody. Max was trying to get the authorities to listen to him about the real aliens.

"We saw them!" Max was yelling as he was taken away. "They were big and . . ."

"Give it a rest, already!" muttered Steve. "No one's going to believe us."

Lester was there, smiling. He believed them.

The Mystery Machine was repaired and the gang was ready to leave, except for Shaggy and Scooby.

"You guys okay?" Fred asked them.

"Like, we're just completely destroyed, is all," Shaggy said sadly.

"Reah, restroyed," Scooby added.

Velma thought she had just the thing to cheer them up. She held up a new box of Scooby Snacks.

Scooby and Shaggy jumped into the Mystery Machine and started gobbling up the Snacks.

"Well, that didn't take long!" Velma said, smiling.

As the van drove away across the desert, Shaggy and Scooby could be heard from a distance.

"Like, hey! It's mine!"

"Ro, rine!"

by Jesse Leon McCann

Scooby-Doo and the rest of the Mystery, Inc. gang were on their way across the desert in the Mystery Machine. It was a hot day and everyone was really thirsty. They were all glad when they spied a small town in the distance.

"Hooray!" they cheered when they spotted a roadside refreshment stand.

"Like, I could really go for a cold soda," Shaggy cried.

"Ree, roo!" Scooby-Doo agreed. He nodded and stuck out his tongue. "*Bleah!*"

As Fred pulled the Mystery Machine off the highway, the gang noticed some sad-looking kids sitting by the stand. It looked like the owner was mad at them.

"You kids are driving me crazy! You're always underfoot," Mr. Reed, the stand owner, growled at the kids. "Find some other place to go."

"Like, why don't you kids beat the heat at that groovy water park over there?" Fred asked.

One boy looked up sadly and said, "We can't. That's my dad's place, and he had to shut it down."

The three kids were named Matt, Amanda, and Ronnie. They told Shaggy and the others that Matt's dad had to sell the park, even though it had been the family business for years.

"But why?" asked Daphne. "You'd think it would be a very popular spot in a hot place like this!"

"It's closed because it's haunted," Amanda said in a quiet voice. "Haunted by spooky water monsters."

"Ha-ha-haunted?" Shaggy said with a gulp.

"Rooky water ronsters?" Scooby whimpered.

"That's right, water monsters!" Mr. Reed grumbled. "They're evil spirits that sometimes possess watery places!"

"The water monsters are half man and half fish," Ronnie told the gang, his eyes wide. "They are white like ghosts and they have sharp teeth!"

"Ghosts are bad for business!" Mr. Reed complained.

"Don't worry, everyone, we'll get to the bottom of this," Fred said, leading the gang into the park. "If there's one thing I love, it's a good mystery."

"Zoinks! Like, if there's one thing I *don't* love, it's ghosts!" Shaggy cried.

"Ree neither!" Scooby agreed.

Suddenly, Scooby's nose sniffed wildly and his tail stuck straight up into the air like an antenna. *Poing!* Shaggy was sniffing, too. "Like, somebody's having a barbecue inside the water park!" he said excitedly.

"Reah! Reah! Rarbecue!" Scooby exclaimed.

"You guys can look for the barbecue that way," Fred told them. "The girls and I will explore over here."

Scooby and Shaggy knew they were getting close to the delicious-smelling barbecue, but they couldn't find it. They checked everywhere. Shaggy yanked open a door, then turned as white as a ghost. Without warning, a scary water creature jumped out at them!

"Grrr!" it growled as it reached for them!

"Zoinks! Let's get out of here, Scoob!" Shaggy shouted. "Like, I think I just lost my appetite for barbecue — especially if we're on the menu!"

MAIN PARK
WATER VALVE

Shaggy and Scooby raced into a nearby tunnel. It was the water control center for the park —
and it came to a dead end!

"Grrr!" The creature was gaining on them.

"Like, no way to go but up, Scoob!" Shaggy said. "Come on!"

Shaggy climbed up the ladder in a flash. But Scooby wasn't getting anywhere. He was climbing
the spokes of a valve wheel, not the ladder! The wheel turned around and around.

"Rooooh!" Scooby-Doo wailed.

Meanwhile, Fred, Daphne, and Velma were checking out the park from above.

"Let's see if we can spot those evil monsters," Fred said.

"Wait, I think I hear something rumbling," Daphne told them. "And it's coming this way!"

Suddenly, a huge surge of water came rushing down the slide. *Whoosh!* The water caught the kids and carried them away at full speed.

Oh, no! Scooby-Doo had accidentally turned on *all* the park's water rides!

Soon the gang found themselves being swept down a twisting tube.

"Jinkies! I like water parks as much as anyone!" Velma shouted. "But I wish I'd had time to put on my bathing suit first!"

Down, down, down they sped — through the slide, around crazy turns and dizzying spirals. (Actually, it was kind of fun!)

Then, just as suddenly as it had begun, the ride ended. The kids found themselves washed into a beautiful lagoon. *Splash!*

Daphne was not happy. "Just look at my hair!" she complained.

"Never mind your hair. Where are my glasses?" Velma asked. "Oh, here they are."

As Velma slid on her specs, she spotted the gang's first clue. There was a strange-looking truck parked next to the lagoon.

"Jeepers," said Daphne. "What's all that equipment in the back of that van? It looks like it's for scientific testing."

Fred nodded. "It is. I've seen that kind of equipment before. It's for locating and testing underground water."

But before they could investigate further, the kids got an unpleasant surprise. A creature from the deep jumped out from behind the truck, growled, and lunged right at them!

At the same time, Shaggy and Scooby were tiptoeing quietly through a dark corridor under the park. "It looks like we lost that growling ghoulie, Scoob," Shaggy whispered. "Like, I think we're safe."

"Roh boy!" Scooby said happily.

But they quickly changed their minds! A giant octopus with big, ugly eyes and sharp, pointy teeth appeared in front of them. It grabbed at them with a long, slimy tentacle!

Shaggy and Scooby fled in the other direction, into a strange round room. They clanged the door shut behind them.

Right away, the guys knew they were in trouble. Water was spraying from the walls, filling the entire chamber. Before long, Shag and Scoob had to dog-paddle to keep their heads above water. Then suddenly, the water was propelling them upward. They looked up — and there was no ceiling, just a long tunnel going up and up!

The two friends hugged each other and gulped.

Scooby and Shaggy shot out the top of the park's volcano. It was like being fired from a water cannon! They were so high up, they could see everything.

"Zoinks! Look, Scoob, there's another monster chasing the rest of the gang!" Shaggy shouted.

But they didn't have time to worry about the others now. For, as fast as they'd gone up, they were now coming *down*!

Luckily, Shaggy and Scooby landed in the volcano's river. It carried them over churning water-falls down to the lagoon at the bottom. They forgot to be scared — they were having too much fun!

"Like, cowabunga, River Doggie!" Shaggy shouted happily. "Ride those rapids, Scoob!"

"Ree-hee-hee!" Scooby laughed.

Shaggy and Scooby finally came to a gentle stop in the lagoon.

"Man, that was one *wild* ride!" Shaggy said.

"Reah! *Rild!*" Scooby-Doo nodded.

"We'd better go find the others," Shaggy suddenly remembered. "They looked like they could use some help!"

The two friends didn't realize it, but at that very moment, *they* needed help, too!

Close by, Fred, Daphne, and Velma were hiding from the water monsters. Now there were *two* creatures from the deep chasing after them!

"Those creatures sure are protective of that truck," Velma said. "It must be a very important clue."

Fred noticed an office door. "Let's hide in here and see if we can figure out this mystery!" he said.

"Hmm," Fred said. "This place doesn't look deserted. In fact, it looks like someone works here every day!"

"I found another clue," Velma said, holding up some blueprints. "I'm beginning to get an idea about what's going on around here."

Before Velma could explain, there was a loud banging on the door. The kids jumped.

"Uh-oh. I think those creatures have found us!" Daphne cried.

But it wasn't the water monsters pounding on the door. It was Shaggy and Scooby-Doo! They were in big trouble! The giant octopus had found them again, and it was trying to wrap them up in its slimy tentacles.

"Like, let us in!" Shaggy shouted.

"Rellllp!" Scooby cried.

Shaggy and Scooby slammed the door before the enormous octopus could reach inside.

"This is no good," Velma said. "That's the only door in or out. We've got to go find more clues if we're going to solve this mystery."

"Like, not me!" Shaggy whimpered. "I'm staying right here, where it's octopus-free!"

"I know what we can do!" Fred said. He pointed to a vent in the wall. "This vent is big enough for us to crawl through. Let's go!"

They all began crawling into the vent. But before Velma climbed in, she spotted another clue. It was a battery charger.

Once the gang had crawled to safety, Fred had an idea. "Shaggy and Scooby, you take this hose," he said. "Try to attract the creatures' attention. When you signal, we'll turn on the water full blast. Hose the monsters into that net and we'll wrap them up!"

"Ruh-uh!" Scooby shook his head from side to side.

"Like, no way, Fred," Shaggy said. "We're not going anywhere near those fishy freaks!"

"Would you do it for a handful of Scooby Snacks?" Velma said, holding the treats in the air. "They're nacho-flavored!"

Shag and Scoob couldn't resist Scooby Snacks — especially nacho ones! Soon they were munching happily as they headed off to hunt for the water monsters.

They hadn't gone far when they made a lucky discovery. It was the barbecue they had smelled earlier!

"Like, my compliments to the chef, whoever he is," Shaggy said between bites. Scooby smiled, nodded, and kept chewing.

Munch! Chomp! They were so busy eating, they didn't notice that three watery creatures had suddenly joined them!

"Turn on the hose! The hose!" Shaggy yelled as they backed away from the angry creatures.

"Rhe rose! Rhe rose!" Scooby joined in.

But the hose filled with pressure too quickly, and Shaggy and Scooby were lifted off the ground and into the air!

"Too much pressure! Too much!" Shaggy yelled.

"Roo ruch! Roo ruch!" Scooby cried.

Shaggy and Scooby hung onto the wild hose with all their might. It shot back and forth through the air like a bucking bronco.

Fred, Daphne, and Velma tried to turn down the water pressure, but the valve wouldn't budge.

"I've got bad news, girls," Fred said. "This valve is stuck."

But before the monsters could get to the others, Scooby and Shaggy came down again. As they fell, the hose wrapped around the monsters, knotting them up so they couldn't get loose. Scooby and Shaggy had saved the day!

"You couldn't have done better if you were cowboys in a rodeo!" Fred said with a grin as he finally managed to turn off the hose.

All the kids laughed. But then . . .

The snarling, slimy octopus returned!

"Roh, no!" Scooby yelled. He jumped into Shaggy's arms. Everyone was terrified! Everyone but Velma.

She calmly walked over to one of their captives and took something away from it. It was a remote control! She twisted a knob, and the giant octopus disappeared!

"Like, I don't get it," said Shaggy. "What happened to the big ugly-pus?"

"It was just a hologram," Velma explained. She pointed to a projector up on the water park mountain.

"And these creatures are just the soda stand owner, Mr. Reed, and a couple of his cronies," Fred said.

"According to the blueprints in the office, there's a big supply of underground water beneath the park," Velma continued. "These crooks wanted to develop this land and build a city where they could control all the water."

"That's why they scared everyone away," Daphne said.

"We would have gotten away with it, too, if it weren't for you meddling kids and your dog," muttered Mr. Reed.

It wasn't long before the water park reopened for the town to enjoy. Matt, Amanda, and Ronnie invited Scooby and the gang back for a big party. They had fun in the sun all day long, splashing in the cool water and sliding down the slides!

"Thanks for saving our park," Matt's dad said to the gang. "As far as I'm concerned, you've all got free lifetime memberships here!"

"Rooby-Doobie-Doo!" cheered Scooby.

SCOOBY-DOO! and the PHANTOM COWBOY

by Jesse Leon McCann

For James Martin, a red-headed fan, his parents' joy

"Yee-haw!" Shaggy cheered, waving his cowboy hat around. "I'm, like, an old cowhand from the Rio Grande, y'all!"

"Ree-raw!" Scooby-Doo joined in, spinning his lasso.

Scooby and his friends from Mystery, Inc., were headed to Phantom Gulch, a real-life western ghost town that had been turned into a theme park.

But when the gang got to Phantom Gulch, they got a big surprise — it was completely deserted. It really *was* a ghost town!

WELCOME TO PHANTOM GULCH

CLOSED FOR GOOD!

THE MYSTERY MACHINE

"Jeepers!" Daphne exclaimed. "Where is everybody?"

The gang didn't have to search for long. The remaining citizens of Phantom Gulch were hiding behind the general store. They were about to leave town for good.

"Sorry, folks!" said the town's sheriff, Matt Taff. "Some kind of an ornery ghost has been chasing everyone out of Phantom Gulch. He won't leave us be!"

"That Phantom Cowboy is one mean feller!" Gertie, the owner of the saloon, said, scowling. "And if you know what's good for you, you'll skeedaddle, too!"

"G-g-ghost?" gulped Shaggy.

"Rhantom Rowboy? *Roh, ro!*" Scooby didn't like the sound of that!

"The Phantom Cowboy has been bothering us for a couple months. We had the worst haunting a few days ago, I reckon," explained Sheriff Matt.

Sheriff Matt said that the creepy cowpoke rode atop a wild, snorting, ghost buffalo! He screamed like a crazy prairie coyote during a full moon. The visitors were so scared, they all left in a hurry and no one had come back since.

"You can't have a tourist attraction without tourists," Sheriff Matt said sadly. "The owners of the town had to close down Phantom Gulch and sell the land to the rancher next door. Now we're all out of work, thanks to that spooky sidewinder!"

"Come on, gang! Let's see if we can get to the bottom of this mystery," Fred suggested.

It wasn't long before they spotted a man who owned the ranch right next door to Phantom Gulch. His name was Harry Parker and he was busy trying to train one of his horses.

"Shucks, kids, them ghosts are mighty fearsome creatures. If I was you, I'd vamoose before they come back again," Mr. Parker exclaimed. "They're always spooking my horses!"

Fred, Shaggy, and Scooby tried to make friends with Mr. Parker's horse. But it snorted and made like it was going to clobber them with its hooves.

"Zoinks! That horse is spooking me!" Shaggy cried.

Despite Mr. Parker's advice, the kids wanted to investigate Phantom Gulch. While the girls went to the courthouse to look for clues, the boys decided to check out the saloon. But on the way there, Scooby spotted something that really scared him.

"Roast racks!" Scooby gulped, grabbed Shaggy, and pointed nervously. "Roast racks! Roast racks!"

"Like, racks of roasts, Scooby?" Shaggy laughed. "Sounds delicious! Where?"

Fred frowned. "Not racks of roasts, Shaggy. *Ghost tracks!*"

"*Zoinks!*" Shaggy exclaimed.

143

Meanwhile, the girls had found something interesting in the courthouse. After rummaging through an old rolltop desk, they discovered the deed to Phantom Gulch.

"That's strange. According to this, Mr. Parker bought the town last week and sold it to Mega Co. Industries yesterday," Velma said. "Now, why would he do that?"

"*Hmm.* Good question," Daphne answered. "Let's go ask him." Daphne tried to open the door, but it wouldn't budge. "Jeepers! It's locked!"

Just then, they heard the shuffle of feet on the other side of the door. Then came a low, ominous laugh. Someone . . . or some*thing* . . . had them trapped inside!

"These are hoof prints, all right," Fred said as he inspected the tracks. "They could belong to the ghost buffalo! Let's see where they lead."

"Like, let's not and say we did," Shaggy said hopefully. "What do you say, Fred, ol' pal?"

"Reah, Red, ol' ral?" Scooby echoed.

Oddly enough, the tracks led right into the saloon. Once they saw there weren't any ghosts there, Shaggy and Scooby thought it was pretty cool to be in a real-life, old west saloon!

"Barkeep!" Shaggy joshed. "We're two tough, ornery hombres! Give us a couple of tall root beers, pardner!"

"Ree-hee-hee-hee!" Scooby giggled.

"Shaggy, stop goofing around and take a look upstairs," Fred said, grinning good-naturedly. "Maybe somebody left a clue in one of the boarding rooms."

"Well, shore thing, feller!" Shaggy lifted the brim of his hat just like a real cowboy. Then he swaggered up the stairs to the second level. "Glad t' oblige y'all, tenderfoot!"

Suddenly, the Phantom Cowboy came charging down the staircase riding his rip-snorting buffalo!

"*Zoinks!* It's the g-g-ghosts! Run!" Shaggy cried. He ran as fast as he could. Meanwhile, the Phantom Cowboy spun a lasso over his head. He was trying to rope Shaggy in!

Shaggy ran down the stairs, across the saloon floor, and out through the double swinging doors. The fearsome ghouls followed close behind!

"Run, Raggy, run!" Scooby hollered.

Daphne and Velma listened at the door till they heard the mysterious footsteps walk away. Then they knew they had to escape from the courthouse so they could warn the boys.

Together, the two girls pushed the rolltop desk under a window. Then Daphne climbed on top and up through the window. Velma clambered up after her.

"It's going to be dark soon," Velma said as they crawled out through the window. "I want to find the guys before the sun sets."

Just then, the ghostly cowboy rode by on his buffalo. "*Yaaaaaah!*" he cried, spurring his creepy creature onward. "*Grrrrrowww!!!*"

"Like, heeeelp!" Shaggy was being pulled behind the buffalo, and it looked like a bumpy ride.

"Jinkies!" cried Velma.

Fred and Scooby-Doo were chasing behind the Phantom Cowboy and his buffalo, trying to rescue Shaggy. The buffalo was fast, however. Just as they were turning a corner and about to disappear from sight, the cowboy turned and pointed at the rest of the gang. "Leave here now!" he called in a booming, eerie voice. "Or I'll come back and get y'all!"

149

By the time the gang reached the corner, the Phantom Cowboy was gone. And so was Shaggy.
"Jeepers! Now what do we do?" Daphne asked.
"Well, it's getting dark," Velma said. "We can't very well look for Shaggy without some sort of light."
"I'll bet there are some lanterns in there." Fred pointed to an old blacksmith's barn down the street. "Let's take a look."
Sure enough, they found a pair of lanterns and soon had them glowing brightly.

Scooby was feeling very down. His best buddy in the whole world had been whisked away by a spooky desperado riding a buffalo. Velma tried to cheer him with Scooby Snacks, but for once Scooby wasn't in the mood.

"Don't worry, Scooby." Daphne patted him on the head. "Now that we've got light, we're sure to find Shaggy."

Scooby looked determined. "Right!" he barked, jumping to his feet. Soon he was hot on the trail of his kidnapped buddy.

SCOOBY SNACKS

It didn't take long for Scooby to catch Shaggy's scent. He bounded down the street after his friend.

"Look at Scooby go!" Velma said, grinning. "Why, I bet if he lived back in the Old West, he would have been a real trailblazer."

Suddenly, Scooby stopped. He'd found a clue!

"Reanut rutter and relly randrich! Rit's Raggy's!" Scooby declared proudly. Then he pointed down the street. "Rhis ray!"

The gang cautiously followed Scooby to an old bakery and a tailor shop. If Shaggy was inside one of them, then the ghosts could be nearby, too.

"We'll look in the tailor shop," Daphne said. "You boys check out the bakery." She and Velma tiptoed to the front of the tailor shop. But just as they stepped inside, their lantern blew out. Velma quickly pulled out a small box and fumbled for a match.

"Hurry, Velma. It's creepy in here without a light," Daphne whispered.

Velma struck the match. In the sudden light, Daphne and Velma saw they were surrounded by strange figures.

"Jinkies!" Velma cried. Then they saw that the strangers were just tailors' mannequins. "*Whew!*"

At the same time, Scooby-Doo and Fred were searching the bakery for any sign of Shaggy. Fred checked the back room while Scooby sniffed the floor near the oven. All the flour and baking powder made him let out a big sneeze.

Just as Scooby sneezed, a big flour sack in the corner jumped. Frowning, Scooby tiptoed to the sack of flour. He sniffed at it. Then he poked at it with his paw. Nervously, Scooby untied the top.

"Zoinks!" cried Shaggy, leaping out, all covered in flour. "Don't hurt me, Mr. Phantom Cowboy, sir!"

Scooby's hair stood on end. "Roh, ro! Raggy's a rhost!"

After much yelling and jumping, Scooby realized it was really his friend, not a ghost. They were so happy, they hugged and danced around, getting flour dust everywhere.

"All right, you two," Daphne said, pointing to a nearby water trough. "Time to clean up."

Scooby and Shaggy happily agreed. Then they ran back into the bakery. There were leftover cakes, pies, and other goodies in there.

"Man, like, there's nothing like some good eats after you've had the wits scared out of you!" Shaggy declared, chomping on a bagel.

"Roo raid rit!" agreed Scooby between bites of cake.

"Well, it looks like everyone's back to normal." Fred grinned. "Now, let's find those ghosts."

But they didn't have to find the ghosts. The ghosts found them!

Out of the darkness emerged the scary rider on his fearsome buffalo. The kids barely dodged out of the way before the ghosts thundered past. Then the cowboy turned his mount around and headed back for another charge. The gang ran for it.

"Ha ha ha ha ha!" cackled the cowboy as he rode down the main street of Phantom Gulch. "I'll give y'all one more chance to leave this place! Now go!"

Then the ghosts disappeared again.

"Well, it's going to take a lot more than that to scare us away." Daphne frowned. "Right, guys?"

"Like, I don't know . . ." Shaggy began.

"Right!" agreed Fred. "Let's see if we can follow those buffalo tracks! We need to catch those ghosts when they're not expecting us."

"Zoinks!" groaned Shaggy. "I was afraid you were going to say that!"

Scooby nodded miserably. "Ree, roo!"

The buffalo tracks led the kids out of town and down a dusty road. After a while, they spotted a campfire burning on a hill. When they got close enough to get a good view, they realized the campfire wasn't on a hill—it was built inside a hill!

"Man, what a crazy apartment!" Shaggy said.

"That's a pueblo, Shaggy," Velma explained. "Certain Native American tribes used to build pueblos to live in long ago."

"It looks like our ghost friends have moved in," Fred said. "Let's see if they're up for some company."

Long ladders were leaning against the side of the pueblo, so the gang had an easy time climbing up. Fred peeked into the apartment. No one was in sight. He motioned the others forward.

When they were all inside, the gang spread out, searching for clues. Velma found an old mural painted by elders of the tribe that had once lived there.

"This is fascinating," Velma told the gang. "This mural tells of the coming of the settlers and the extinction of the buffalo. According to legend, a mighty phantom will rise up with his ghostly buffalo and curse the descendants of the settlers forever!"

"But if this cowboy is a ghost, why does he need a campfire at night?" Fred pondered. "Something doesn't add up."

159

"Like, who cares?" Shaggy was hugging Scooby tightly. "Now that we know the Phantom Cowboy and his creepy critter are the curse-ers, let's fly this coop before we become the curse-ees!"

"Reah! Reah!" Scooby nodded.

"Too late!" bellowed a booming voice. The ghoulish cowboy and his stamping, snorting buffalo sidekick appeared out of nowhere.

As quick as a wink, the gang scrambled back down the ladders to the bottom of the pueblo. They thought that they'd lost the ghostly duo. But all of a sudden, the ghouls appeared from behind a huge boulder and the chase was on again!

Back through the desert the cowboy chased them. Back through the town of Phantom Gulch he rode after them, laughing, whooping, and hollering all the while.

In fact, the ghosts didn't let up until they'd chased the kids all the way back to the Mystery Machine. When he thought he had finally scared the gang away, the cowboy reared up on his buffalo and rode off in a cloud of dust.

But Fred and the girls weren't about to give up so easily.

"There's got to be a logical explanation for this Phantom Cowboy mystery!" Velma exclaimed.

"The only way we'll get to the bottom of this is by catching that ghost, and I've got an idea how," Fred declared. He looked at Shaggy and Scooby. "Of course, we'll need some bait."

"Like, no way, Fred!" Shaggy cried. "I've had my fill of creepy cowboy curses for one night!"

"Right!" Scooby stuck out his tongue. "Bleah! Reepy cowboy rurses!"

After several minutes of wrangling for Scooby Snacks, Shaggy and Scooby agreed to help catch the ghosts. Velma and Daphne took them back to the tailor shop and dressed them like Old West lawmen.

While Fred and the girls went to set up the trap, Shaggy and Scooby went looking for the Phantom Cowboy and his buffalo. The two ghosts had set up a camp in the desert right outside of town. Taking deep breaths for courage, Shaggy and Scooby moseyed right up to the campfire.

"Howdy, Deputy Scoobert! Do y'all see what I see?" Shaggy said in his best cowboy voice. "A coupla mangy varmints having a weenie-roast without a campfire permit!"

"I think we should run these rascals into the pokey!" Shaggy continued. "Wouldn't y'all agree, Deputy Scoobert?"

"Right, Rarshal Raggy," Scooby answered.

The Phantom Cowboy and his ghost buffalo looked at them in surprise for a minute. Then looks of anger came over their faces. They growled and howled at Shaggy and Scooby.

"Like, on the other hand, maybe we should just let them go with a warning this time," Shaggy called as he turned and bolted away. "Run, Scooby-Doo!"

"Roh-oh-oh!" Scooby cried as he raced away from the campfire.

Scooby-Doo and Shaggy fled through the desert, over brambles and around big boulders. They tried hiding behind cacti and running with the tumbleweeds. But no matter what they did, the Phantom Cowboy and his ghostly buffalo stayed right on their heels.

Finally, with no other choice left, the two friends started climbing a small hill nearby. But it was no use — the ghosts stayed right with them. And Scooby and Shaggy were quickly running out of steam!

When Scooby and Shaggy reached the top of the slope, they realized the hill suddenly ended with a sharp dropoff. They were trapped!

"Oh, no!" Shaggy cried.

This made the Phantom Cowboy laugh with evil delight. "I told y'all to vamoose from these here parts." The ghost grinned. "Now it's too late for you!"

"Like, this is it, old pal," Shaggy said to Scooby. "Happy trails!"

"Ro long, Raggy!" Tears came to Scooby's eyes. "Roh, roo hoo hoo!"

But just as the Phantom Cowboy and the ghost buffalo were about to nab Shaggy and Scooby, the villains fell through a hole in the ground. It was a trap—a hole that Fred, Daphne, and Velma had camouflaged with weeds and grass. The hole was carved into the roof of the pueblo to let the smoke from campfires drift out.

Daphne, Fred, and Velma were waiting underneath the hole with a big net, ready to catch the villains. The Phantom Cowboy and the ghost buffalo dropped right into it, as pretty as you please!

"Now, let's see who was behind this mystery." Fred pulled the mask off the captured Phantom Cowboy.

It was Mr. Parker! He had been pretending to be the Phantom Cowboy all along. The ghost buffalo had actually been his ornery horse in disguise.

"Mr. Parker scared away all the people in Phantom Gulch so he could buy the property real cheap," Velma explained as state troopers arrived to take Mr. Parker away. "Then he sold the town for a huge profit to a big company that wanted to build an even bigger western amusement park."

"I would've gotten away with it, too, if it weren't for you meddlin' kids and your dad-burned dog!" sneered Parker.

"Once the judge finds out what Parker did, the town will revert back to its rightful owners," Daphne said, smiling.

Not too long after that, the townspeople who worked at Phantom Gulch returned to their old jobs. Soon visitors started coming back and the town was a lively, old western tourist attraction again.

"We can't thank you enough for solving the mystery and saving Phantom Gulch!" said Sheriff Matt gratefully. "You kids are real western heroes!"

"Like, shucks, Sheriff . . . 't'weren't nothin' any real western heroes couldn't have done," Shaggy drawled. "As long as they had a pardner like Scooby-Doo!"

"Scooby-Dooby-Doo!" cheered Scooby.

Based on the screenplay
"*Scooby-Doo and the Witch's Ghost*"
by **Davis Doi** & **Glenn Leopold**

Adapted by **Gail Herman**
Story by **Rick Copp** & **David Goodman**

Scooby-Doo and his friends were in a museum disguised as exhibits! They were trying to solve a mystery about warrior mummies.

Suddenly the friends spied the mummies. They were about to uncover the culprits behind the mystery — when someone else did it for them!

The mysterious hero?

"Ben Ravencroft!" Velma cried, "the horror writer!"

The famous writer knew the Mystery, Inc. gang, too. Ben told them that he happened to be at the museum doing research for a book. "I've always admired *your* mystery-solving work," he said to Scooby and his friends. Then he added, "I'm going to my hometown of Oakhaven this weekend. It's so peaceful, why don't you come?"

"Reah!" said Scooby.

But Oakhaven wasn't peaceful at all. Traffic snarled the streets and tourists scurried to buy T-shirts at Mr. McKnight's drugstore.

Ben read from a shirt: "I met the ghost of Oakhaven." What was *that* about?

"Ghost?" said Shaggy. "Rhost?" echoed Scooby. Was there really a ghost in Oakhaven?

Just then Mayor Corey hurried over. "That's not just any ghost," he explained to the gang. "That's the ghost of Sarah Ravencroft. She's one of Ben's ancestors. We must have disturbed her spirit when we built our Puritan Village."

The townspeople had built a model village for tourists to visit — one that looked centuries old, with houses, shops, and people dressed in Puritan costumes. Mayor Corey proudly showed everyone the sights — including old-fashioned prison stocks. Shaggy got into the spirit right away. Pretending to be locked up, he cried, "Look, Scoob! I've been caught!"

Scooby grinned, then took a turn with an old butter churn . . . only he didn't stir it to turn milk into butter. He played it like a guitar. Suddenly he dropped the churn.

"Ropher!" cried Scooby, chasing a gopher down a hole. A moment later he popped back up. He had lost the gopher, but found a small rusty buckle.

"Too bad Scooby didn't find Sarah Ravencroft's journal," Ben told the gang. "She was accused of being a witch. That book would clear our family name."

The gang looked around the village. They walked past a turkey pen and a pumpkin patch. Then Shaggy and Scooby strolled over to Oakhaven Restaurant for lunch. The owner, Jack, read them all the items on the menu.

Shaggy's mouth watered. "Sounds great," he said. "Like give us two of everything!"

Meanwhile, at Ben Ravencroft's mansion, Daphne, Fred, and Velma stared wide-eyed at the horror writer's gruesome knickknacks and pictures. Fred wandered over to a portrait — a young Puritan woman, grasping a journal, standing by a tall oak tree. He read the nameplate: "Sarah Ravencroft."

Velma stepped closer. So *this* was the ancestor whose ghost was now haunting the town.

Ben saw Velma staring at the picture. "Sarah was a Wiccan," Ben explained, "a kind of medicine woman, like a doctor."

"I've read about them," Velma said. "Wiccans don't use ordinary medicine. They understand the forces of nature — herbs and plants — and use them for healing."

"Sarah treated her patients under a large oak tree," Ben went on. "I've searched for that tree around town, hoping to find Sarah's journal, which may have been buried there. But I haven't come up with a thing."

A few minutes later, everyone went to meet Shaggy and Scooby. At the Oakhaven Restaurant, shocked customers were watching the friends chow down — it was like nothing they'd ever seen!

Scooby chomped at a giant hambone. Shaggy stuffed handfuls of fries into his mouth. "Is there anything left in the kitchen?" Velma joked, eyeing the plates piled high with bones and leftovers.

"Let's go and see if that ghost makes an appearance tonight," Fred said to Shaggy and Scooby.

The two friends stared, frightened, at each other. "Like we'd love to," Shaggy told his friends. "But we haven't had dessert yet."

So Ben took Velma, Daphne, and Fred around town trying to spot the ghost, while Shaggy and Scooby gobbled down twelve pies. Finally they staggered out of the restaurant. It was nighttime now, and the dark street was empty.

Thud, thud. Suddenly, loud, heavy footsteps sounded. Shabby and Scooby stopped short. Who was coming?

Three shadowy shapes glided over to them.

"Girls!" Shaggy exclaimed, slicking back his hair. "Hi!" The girls paused under a streetlight. They wore dark, somber clothes. Their faces were deathly pale, and their hair was long and straggly. "Hi," the girls replied with wicked grins. Each one had sharp, jagged teeth!

"I thought there was only *one* witch's ghost!" Shaggy panted as he and Scooby raced away.

All at once, a powerful wind whipped down the street. Leaves swirled and trees shook with the force. The witch's ghost appeared! She looked just like Shaggy imagined, with a pointy hat and cackling voice.

"This town ruined me," shrieked the ghost. "And now it will pay!"

She raised one arm. A red-hot fireball shot out from her fingertips.

Scooby and Shaggy took off. The witch's ghost tossed another fireball, and Shaggy leaped into the air. He held onto Scooby as they raced around the corner — careening straight into Velma, Daphne, Fred, and Ben Ravencroft.

"Ritch's rhost!" cried Scooby.

"Witch's ghost!" Velma repeated. "*You* saw her! Where?" Shaggy led everyone back to the spot, babbling about fireballs and three other witches.

Velma switched on a flashlight. "Hmmm," she said, kneeling to examine some powder. "Fireballs . . ."

"Ahhhh!" A wailing sound echoed through town and strange green lights flickered in the distance.

The gang and Ben tracked the sound and lights to a large clearing in the woods. A stage stood at one end, with three figures swaying under a strange green light show. The noise was music!

"Zoinks!" said Shaggy. "It's those other witches!"

"It's just a band," Fred said. He pointed to a sign that said "Hex Girls" behind the girls. "I heard they're putting on a concert tomorrow night. They must be rehearsing."

No longer scared, Shaggy and Scooby danced to the music. The song ended, and the girls introduced themselves as Thorn, Luna, and Dusk. Fred whispered to Velma, "These girls seem suspicious. Daphne and I will keep an eye on them."

Velma wanted to do more exploring, so she led the others to the witch's ghost spot. "Tire tracks!" she exclaimed, shining her flashlight on some marks in the dirt. "Let's see where they lead!"

Everyone followed the tracks to a large barn. "Shh!" said Velma, pulling everyone into the shadows as a man hurried out. It was the mayor!

"Jinkies!" said Velma, surprised. The barn doors were now padlocked shut, so Ben hoisted her up to a window and she climbed inside. A truck stood in the center of the barn. Its engine was still warm. Why would someone drive a construction truck at night? Velma wondered.

Meanwhile, Shaggy and Scooby followed the mayor. They tried to be quiet, but Mayor Corey stopped and whirled around. The street was empty. So he shrugged and walked on. He didn't notice the guys hiding inside a broken mailbox.

185

A few minutes later, Shaggy and Scooby watched the mayor take a package from a shopkeeper. Then they trailed him to a hotel, where he delivered the package to the owner.

"Zoinks!" Shaggy whispered. "This mayor is one busy guy!"

"Reah!" Scooby agreed.

Shaggy and Scooby continued to follow the mayor around town. But they lost sight of him near an old warehouse.

"Ahhhh!" A loud moan echoed down from the roof, and suddenly the witch's ghost appeared! She swooped toward the guys, reaching out for them with clawed hands.

Scooby and Shaggy tried to run. They spun their legs wildly, but that only made them dig a hole in the dirt. They couldn't get out!

"This town will pay!" the witch's ghost moaned again.

"Send them a bill!" Shaggy yelled back as they finally scrambled free. "But leave *us* alone!"

The guys raced right past their friends and squeezed into another mailbox, quivering with fear. "So what happened?" Velma asked the shaking mailbox.

Shaggy explained everything. Then Fred described a strange ceremony the Hex Girl named Thorn had performed. She had crushed plants and flowers to make some sort of potion.

Velma thought a moment. A phone call would have to be made, and then . . .

"I can solve the mystery," she declared, "and we can leave."

Leave! Shaggy, then Scooby popped free of the mailbox and hugged Velma with joy.

"But I need one more clue," she added.

Back at the concert stage, Velma whispered her plan to the gang. Fred and Daphne nodded, then scurried into the woods. But Shaggy and Scooby were more interested in putting on a show.

"Hey!" Thorn hissed, suddenly appearing behind the pals. She bared her fangs menacingly.

Scooby gulped. "Rorry!"

"Thanks for coming," Velma said, hurrying to greet the spooky musicians.

"But why did you call us?" Thorn asked. "What are we doing here?"

All at once, a blast of wind hit the stage. The witch's ghost was back!

"Runnnnn!" Shaggy cried, his hair standing on end. The ghost hurled a fireball. Everyone scrambled off stage, with the witch's ghost close behind.

It was going just the way Velma had planned. Now to catch the ghost! Suddenly Velma flung herself to the ground, pretending to trip. The ghost screeched to a stop.

"Now!" Velma shouted into the woods.

A tree branch sprang forward, snapping a wire in two. The ghost flew backward out of control — straight into a net hung between two bushes. Velma had set a trap!

Daphne and Fred came out from behind the bushes. Fred looked at the ghost, who was trapped and moaning in the net.

"Let's see who this is," he said. He pulled off the witch mask.

Everyone gasped. "Like, it's the T-shirt guy!" Shaggy exclaimed. "Mr. McKnight!" He was the man who ran the drugstore and, as it turned out, he was also Thorn's father.

"Daddy!" said Thorn.

"I can explain what happened," Velma said. "Mr. McKnight got the fireball powder from Thorn's stage props."

Then she pointed to the truck. It was the same one she'd seen in the barn. Now it was parked in the woods next to a giant fan. "The truck has a wire device that made the ghost fly. The fan created the wind. So it took more than one person to pull off this scam."

Jack the restaurant owner stepped out of the darkness, followed by the hotel owner, the shopkeeper, and finally the mayor. They hung their heads, ashamed.

"These people made money from the tourists who came to see the 'ghost,'" Velma said.

"And *we're* not witches," one Hex Girl told them, taking out her fake fangs. "We just pretend for our act. But Thorn really is a Wiccan. She even makes herbal drinks to soothe our throats for singing."

So *that* was the potion!

"We found Sarah's gravestone when we built our Puritan Village," the mayor went on. "We remembered how she'd been accused of witchcraft. So we used her as our ghost. But we didn't find that journal."

Velma thought back to the portrait in Ben's home. Sarah stood in front of an old oak tree, holding a book that had a buckle. The buckle was just like the one Scooby had found when he chased that gopher down a hole — right by the stump of an oak tree! "And where there's a buckle," Velma told herself, "maybe there's a book!"

Immediately, she dangled two Scooby Snacks in front of Scooby and told him to find the hole. He raced to the spot — and dug up a strange-looking book.

Ben grabbed it. He grinned, but it was an evil grin that darkened his face. "This isn't a journal," he growled in a low, threatening voice. "It's a spellbook. Sarah *was* a witch!"

Velma gasped. He had known it all along!

"And I set up the museum meeting," he told the gang, "so you could help me find it!"

Ben had tricked them all — the gang from Mystery, Inc., the mayor and his friends, the Hex Girls. And now, his evil plans were about to unfold.

"I will summon Sarah," Ben cried. "Together we will rule the world!"

The book glowed red. The wind whipped fiercely, pushing everyone back. The townspeople flew into the stocks of the Puritan Village, and the Hex Girls were tied to a post. Thunder boomed. Lightning flashed. Clouds shifted, and suddenly the witch's ghost — the *real* witch's ghost — swept through the sky.

"Serve me!" Ben commanded.

But the witch's ghost had *other* ideas! "I serve no one!" She glared at Ben, holding out her arm. A fire blast shot out and caught Ben up in a green glowing ball.

The spellbook dropped to the ground. "We need that book," Velma whispered to Shaggy and Scooby.

"Get close to that evil bad guy Ben?" Shaggy groaned. But he and Scooby dashed away while the witch flung fireball after fireball at the others.

"The Wiccans imprisoned me in the book!" Sarah shrieked. "And no one will do that again!"

One blast zapped the pumpkin patch. Boom! The pumpkins exploded and changed into monster creatures, skittering on vine-legs. "Jinkies!" cried Velma, as she sped quickly away.

For a second, the coast was clear, so Shaggy grabbed the book. But the witch's ghost sent one more fireball. It crashed into the turkey pen. "Get them, birds," she ordered.

"Even we're not scared of that," Shaggy said. Only suddenly the turkey grew into a huge monstrous creature. "Like now we are!" said Shaggy.

He and Scooby raced into a museum building, and rushed out in Puritan costumes. Shaggy held a giant turkey baster while Scooby held a bowl of stuffing. "Uh-oh!" squawked the turkey, turning tail to run.

"Thou will not escape!" the witch's ghost cackled. She gripped Scooby by the tail, holding him upside down.

"Zoinks!" cried Shaggy, jumping out of his costume. He flung a bucket of water at the witch's ghost — just like Dorothy had done in *The Wizard of Oz.*

"Hey!" he said, surprised. "Like you're not melting!" He tossed the bucket and it landed on the witch's head. She dropped Scooby. "Raggy, run!" cried Scooby as the bucket popped free.

Shaggy grabbed the witch's spellbook and threw it to Velma. She flipped through the pages, searching for a spell to imprison Sarah.

"Here!" she said to Thorn. "You're a Wiccan. Read it!"

The witch was getting closer! Quickly Thorn read, "Ancient evil get thee hence . . ."

Suddenly the book jumped out of Thorn's hand, glowing and crackling with energy. The wind died away and Sarah's ghost was sucked into its pages. "I won't go back alone!" she cried, grabbing Ben's foot. Whoosh! They disappeared inside the spellbook — together.

That night, the Hex Girls along with Shaggy and Scooby performed their concert to a sell-out crowd. The giant turkey never returned to its regular size, and tourists were still flocking to Oakhaven to see it. The mayor and townspeople grinned happily.

"Scooby-dooby-doo," Scooby hissed and grinned back, showing off his brand-new fangs.

SCOOBY-DOO!™
and the FANTASTIC PUPPET FACTORY

by Jesse Leon McCann

Scooby-Doo and his Mystery, Inc., pals were at the malt shop. Fred and Daphne were getting the gang some goodies while Velma listened to the radio.

"This just in," the radio blared. "The national bank was robbed this evening by the Black Mask Bandits! This is the fifth bank they've hit in a week. The police are baffled."

"Jinkies!" Velma said. "I hope they catch those thieves soon."

"Like, I just hope Fred got us some triple-fudge cheesecake sundaes with extra strawberry sauce on top!" Shaggy said.

"Reah! Reah!" agreed Scooby hungrily.

Just then, the gang was joined by Mrs. Jenkins, a kindly old lady who lived down the street. She looked really worried.

"I'm so glad I found you kids," Mrs. Jenkins said. "Teddy, my poor kitty, is missing. Won't you find him for me?"

"Man, that's the kind of mystery I dig the most — no ghosts, ghoulies, or goblins!" said Shaggy bravely. "Like, don't worry, Mrs. J. We'll find Teddy for you!"

"Oh, thank you!" said Mrs. Jenkins gratefully. "I last saw him in front of that abandoned puppet factory on the corner of Pitman Street."

The gang looked up and down the street for Teddy. As they were searching, they met two security guards, Biff and Bob.

"We were hired to patrol all the buildings on this street," Biff told them. "But we haven't seen any black-and-white cats."

"I'd stay away from that old puppet factory if I were you," said Bob. "We keep hearing strange noises around there, like it's haunted or something."

"H-H-H-Haunted?" Shaggy cried. "Maybe we should look for Teddy somewhere else — like at home in bed, under the covers!"

"Ruh-huh!" Scooby nodded and gulped. "Ret's go!"

"I think we should check in the alley." Velma explained, "Cats like to hang out there."

They looked under big cardboard boxes and in Dumpsters. They called Teddy's name softly. But suddenly, a window in the building next door flew open and a woman stuck out her head.

"Quiet!" she screeched. "I'm sick of all the comings and goings through that door at all hours of the day and night!"

"Hey, look!" Fred said as the woman slammed the window shut. "The factory door *is* open. Let's take a look inside. Teddy might have wandered in and gotten trapped."

The factory was a little spooky inside. Many of the puppets looked almost real in the moonlight.

"Let's split up," Fred said. "I'll go this way with Daphne and Velma. Shaggy, you check that way with Scooby-Doo."

But Shaggy and Scooby didn't want to split up. They were still worried about the guards' warning.

"You know," said Daphne, "this place hasn't been closed very long. I'll bet there's still food around here someplace."

"Why didn't you say so?" Shaggy cried cheerfully. "C'mon, Scooby, let's take a look around!"

"There's got to be a refrigerator around here someplace," Shaggy told Scooby as they searched the ware-house.

"Reah! Refrigerator!" Scooby said, sniffing for food.

"I wonder what happened to the owner of this place," Shaggy said. "Like, I heard he had to close down because he lost all his money gambling."

But before Scooby could answer, an eerie voice called out from a little stage nearby — a puppet stage!

"Ladies and gentlemen!" said the voice. "Presenting the hilarious and haunting Punch and Judy Show!"

The weird puppets on the little stage did a play. "Hoo-hoo! I'm going to get you!" warned one puppet, Mr. Punch. *Wham!* He hit a girl puppet on the head.

"Boo-hoo! I'm going to get you!" cried Judy, the other puppet. *Wham!* Judy hit Mr. Punch back.

The two puppets laughed and disappeared. Then, all of the sudden, a bunch of puppets popped up behind Shaggy and Scooby. Mr. Punch popped back up and pointed at them.

"No! no! no! I know what we'll do!" cackled Mr. Punch. "We're *haunted* puppets and we're going to get *you!*"

Scooby and Shaggy tried to get away, but the puppets followed close behind.

"Hee-hee-hee!" Mr. Punch laughed. "Look who I see!"

The puppets swung at Shaggy and Scooby with their little clubs. Shaggy and Scooby grabbed some empty paint cans and put them on their heads as helmets.

"Zoinks! Like, this bunch of haunted puppets has a burning desire to see us clubbed, Scoob!" Shaggy cried.

"Ri know! Ri know!" Scooby bellowed as they ran wildly through the warehouse.

Meanwhile, Fred and the girls were searching another area of the factory. Velma found an important clue on the floor.

"Look at this!" Velma said. "Paperwork for shipping puppet heads to Tahiti. It has today's date on it!"

Before Velma could say more, a spotlight came on, shining right in Fred's, Daphne's, and Velma's eyes. It was coming from a platform above, where a ventriloquist's dummy was sitting.

"Greetings," the dummy said, all by himself. "I'm afraid you've come to the wrong place at the wrong time!"

The talking dummy wasn't the gang's only surprise. Mrs. Jenkins' cat, Teddy, was sitting on its lap.

"Who are you?" asked Daphne. "What do you want?"

"I am the leader of the haunted puppets," the dummy said. "We turn anyone who comes into our warehouse into haunted puppets, too!"

"We don't believe in haunted puppets," Fred said. "Whatever you're up to, you won't get away with it!"

"We'll see about that!" The dummy laughed as he pulled a switch. Before Fred, Daphne, and Velma could get out of the way, a cage dropped from the ceiling and trapped them inside!

The dummy pulled a few more switches. Wires dropped from the ceiling. On the ends of the wires were claws that grabbed the gang by their arms and lifted them up into the air. The wires picked up and put down the gang over and over again, making their arms and legs dance wildly.

"Dance! Dance!" laughed the dummy. "Now you know how a puppet feels. Soon you will be a puppet, too, when I cast my haunting spell on you! Ha-ha-ha!"

Fred, Daphne, and Velma started to worry they might be dancing like that forever!

At the same time, Shaggy and Scooby-Doo were thinking they'd lost the creepy Mr. Punch and his crew. They were hiding in the costume room. But when they stopped to take a breath, Mr. Punch popped out at them again.

"Hee-hee-hee! You can't lose me!" giggled Mr. Punch. "I am Mr. Punch, you see?"

"Like, run, Scoob, run!" Shaggy cried.

"Ri am running!" Scooby yelped.

Shaggy and Scooby didn't know it, but they were heading right into the arms — or legs — of danger! Creepy spider puppets were coming for them!

Crash! Scooby-Doo and Shaggy collided with the huge spiders. They all fell to the ground in a pile.

"Help! Help!" Shaggy yelled. "These hairy horrors have me trapped in their web!"

"Ree too! Ree too!" cried Scooby.

Shaggy stopped kicking. "Hey, look, Scoob," he said. "These puppets aren't moving! I guess they're not the haunted kind."

"Roh, yeah," Scooby said, relieved.

Then they noticed, happily, that Mr. Punch had vanished.

But they didn't have much time to relax, because . . .

. . . a giant dragon puppet was headed straight for them!

It roared and breathed fire as it flew over their heads. Then it turned and swung back around, aiming right for Scoob and Shag!

Scooby and Shaggy ran — straight into a wall! Slowly, they turned around and looked right into the eyes of the ferocious dragon.

"Like, good-bye, ol' pal," said Shaggy. "I guess this dragon is going to have himself a Shaggy and Scooby-Doo barbecue!"

"Roh, noooooo!" Scooby cried and covered his eyes with his paws.

BOOOOOOSH! The dragon blew fire at them!

Meanwhile, the dummy had left Fred, Daphne, and Velma hanging from the wires. They could hear him laughing in the distance.

"We've got to find a way to get down from here," Fred said.

"I've got an idea," said Daphne. She reached around carefully and took off one of her shoes. Then she threw it toward the wall. The shoe hit one of the switches near the dummy's platform. In a split second, Fred was released from the wires.

"Good shot, Daphne!" Fred cheered. "I'll have you two down in no time."

"We've got to warn Shaggy and Scooby about that crazy dummy," Daphne said, once they were all free.

"Hey, I think I've found another clue," said Velma, looking at a puppet head she'd pulled from a crate. "This head has money stuffed inside it! Why would someone do that?"

Instead of an answer, the gang got a big surprise! Mr. Punch and some other puppets popped out from behind the crate.

"More visitors? Well, well, well!" Mr. Punch sneered. "We'll get them here and now, so they'll not tell!"

"Run, gang!" Fred yelled.

The gang quickly hurried away, leaving the puppets behind. Luckily, they escaped in the nick of time.

"You got away, tee-hee, tee-hee!" Mr. Punch cackled. "But we'll get you, wait and see!"

"What are we going to do now?" asked Velma.

"I think the answer is right in front of us," Fred said, pointing. "Look, it's Biff and Bob, the night watchmen. They'll help us."

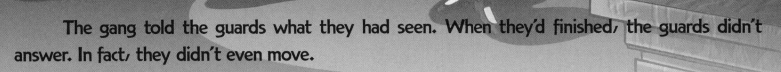

The gang told the guards what they had seen. When they'd finished, the guards didn't answer. In fact, they didn't even move.

"What's wrong with them?" Daphne asked worriedly.

"I'll tell you," said a creepy voice from behind them.

When Fred, Daphne, and Velma turned around, they were face-to-face with the dummy, Mr. Punch, and their crew once more.

"We've turned them into puppets," said the dummy.

"Yes, indeed, indeedy do!" laughed Mr. Punch. "And now we'll turn you into puppets, too!"

Meanwhile, the dragon had almost caught up with Shaggy and Scooby. But before it could blast them with its fiery breath, they dropped to the ground and crawled under its belly. They ran with all their might, trying to lose the huge, beastly puppet.

Then, all at once, Shaggy and Scooby tripped over an old dummy lying on the ground. They flew through the air and landed in a rolling cart. The cart took off like a shot. It was moving so fast, they'd soon left the dragon far behind.

"Rook out!" Scooby cried. There was a lion in the cart! But it was just a puppet head. Scooby quickly tossed it away.

"Like, gangway!" Shaggy hollered as the cart zipped along.

Just as the dummy and his puppets were reaching for Fred, Daphne, and Velma, their friends Shaggy and Scooby raced by in the rolling cart.

"Like, anybody need a ride?" Shaggy cried.

Fred, Daphne, and Velma leaped into the cart. They all sped away from the angry puppets.

"Nice going, Shaggy and Scooby," Fred said as they all raced along. "I only have one question — how do we stop this thing?"

"I was afraid you were going to ask that!" said Shaggy.

"ROOOOOOH!" Scooby moaned.

Crash! The cart ran into a wall and tipped the whole gang onto the floor.

"Well, it was a bumpy way to escape, but I guess we're okay," Daphne said as they got to their feet.

"Never mind the bumps!" Shaggy said. "Look, snacks!"

"Roh boy, roh boy!" Scooby cheered.

"The machine's out of order. I'll just leave the money in the coin return," Shaggy explained, reaching his arm into the vending machine.

"Look at these pictures," Velma said. "Someone who worked here spends a lot of time on the beach."

Suddenly, the dragon appeared overhead and let out a scorching blast!

Shaggy wanted to run, but his hand was stuck! Scooby grabbed him and tugged with all his might. But Shaggy wouldn't budge.

"Zoinks! Pull, Scoob!" Shaggy begged. "Pull like you've never pulled before!"

"Ri'm pulling, ri'm pulling!" Scooby cried.

At last Shaggy's hand came free. He and Scooby stumbled backward, accidentally hitting a nearby switch.

All of a sudden, the dragon stopped. The gang looked up at it. It was just sitting still in midair.

"Look, it was just a puppet on a rail!" Daphne exclaimed.

"And the fire the dragon was breathing was probably created with some of these Chinese New Year fireworks," Velma added.

"I'm beginning to think those puppets aren't as haunted as they seem," Fred told them. "I think we should set a trap for them."

Fred had an idea how to distract the puppets. He wanted Scooby and Shaggy to dress up as acrobats, jump around, and wave sparklers in the air. When they got the attention of the puppets, Fred and the girls would sneak up on the puppets and surprise them.

"Like, no way, Fred!" said Shaggy. "I don't want to end up as a haunted puppet!"

"Ree, neither!" Scooby said.

"Would you do it for a Scooby Snack?" Velma pulled out a box. "They're double-butterscotch flavor!"

Moments later, Scooby-Doo and Shaggy were all dressed up and dancing around, sparklers in hand and paw. Sure enough, the haunted puppets were there in a flash.

"I don't know what game you're playing," the dummy puppet leader said angrily, "but the time has come to lock you up and turn you into puppets!"

"Like, I think the time has come for us to run away," Shaggy said nervously. "Are you with me, Scoob?"

"Ruh-uh." Scooby shook his head. "Ri'm in front of you!"

Just as Scooby and Shaggy started to flee, three policemen appeared out of nowhere.

"Everybody freeze!" shouted one of the policemen.

"Everybody run!" shouted the dummy.

Teddy the cat, who had been sitting quietly nearby, was frightened by all the noise. He jumped right on Scooby's head. Scooby tripped and fell toward the box of fireworks. Shaggy tried to catch Scooby and Teddy, but he went tumbling, too.

As they fell, one of the sparklers fell into the box of fireworks. It lit a fuse, and . . .

Boom! Bang! Blam!

The fireworks went off, exploding in colorful lights and patterns all over the factory.

"Don't shoot! Don't shoot!" someone yelled. "We give up!"

A bunch of men ran out from behind the boxes and crates. They all had enormous puppets on their hands.

"We confess!" said a man with the dummy on his arm. "We're the bank robbers! We did it!"

"All right! Don't move!" said one of the policemen. "Shaggy, tie up these criminals!"

"There, all tied up and prison-bound!" said Shaggy when he had finished the last knot. "But how do you cops know my name?"

"Because we're not really policemen," Fred said as he, Daphne, and Velma stood up, holding the policemen in their arms. "These are puppets. We found them in the costume room, and we realized they'd be perfect for tricking whoever was working the haunted puppets."

"The two guards are actually puppets," Velma explained. "The haunted puppets are really the bank robbers, the owner of this factory and his men. They were going to smuggle all the money they'd stolen out of the country and live in the tropics."

"They made up the haunted puppet story to keep people away while they robbed banks," Daphne said as the real police took the robbers away.

"We would have gotten away with our plan, too, if it weren't for you pesky kids and that dog!" growled the owner of the puppet factory.

"Just think, we solved another mystery *and* returned Teddy to Mrs. Jenkins," Fred said.

Mrs. Jenkins was overjoyed. "I'm the happiest woman in town, thanks to you kids!"

Shaggy smiled. "And no strings attached, thanks to Scooby-Doo!"

"Rooby-Dooby-Doo!" cheered Scooby-Doo.

FUN TIME PUPPET CO.

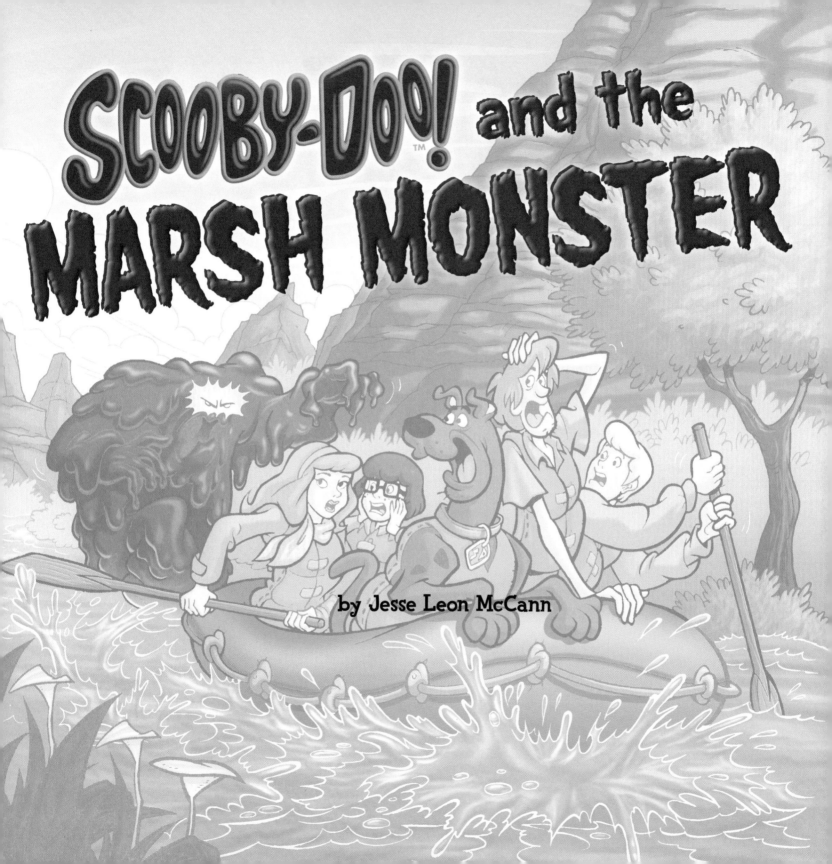

SCOOBY-DOO! and the MARSH MONSTER

by Jesse Leon McCann

For Dee and Teri Masters; nights of Punch, Judy,
and bursting into flame

Scooby-Doo and his pals from Mystery, Inc., were about to start their summer rafting vacation — on the river wild! They were renting equipment from Mr. Samuels, a kindly old gentleman.

The gang was all set to have a lot of fun. But then they met some unhappy river rafters who had just had a horrible experience!

RAPID RIVER
RAFTING COMPANY

The rafters introduced themselves. Their names were Jemma, Martin, and Ben.

"We were supposed to float down the river for three days, and camp on the shore of the river each night," Jemma said.

"On the second day, we were attacked by a terrible monster!" Ben exclaimed.

"Zoinks!" cried Shaggy. "A m-m-monster?!"

"R-r-ronster?" Scooby gulped.

"A big, oily monster!" exclaimed Martin. "It looked like a man, but it was covered from head to toe with something slimy and sludgy!"

"It gave an evil roar and knocked us into the water," Jemma said. "We were so scared, we hightailed it back here right away!"

"Oh, I'm so sorry this happened to you," exclaimed Mr. Samuels. "I'll give you a full refund, don't you worry!"

"We're sorry, Mr. Samuels, but we can't continue coming here if we have to worry about strange creatures attacking us," Martin said sadly. The disappointed campers packed up their car and drove away.

Just then, a pair of men who were hiking by stopped to talk to Mr. Samuels. The leader of the pair was a very rich man named Jeremiah Peabody. With him was his assistant, Hank.

"Tough luck, old sport." Peabody smiled at Mr. Samuels. "If your business is being ruined by this marsh monster, perhaps you should reconsider my offer. Sell your land to me. It might save you a lot of grief."

"Oh, no!" Mr. Samuels said sadly. "What am I going to do? I don't want to sell my land to Peabody. I just know he'll turn this place into a toxic dump for his factories!"

"Don't worry, Mr. Samuels," Fred assured him. "We'll solve this marsh monster mystery for you!"

"Like, no way, Fred!" cried Shaggy. "I'm not going near any marshes or monsters! And I'm sure not going near any marsh monsters!"

"Ree reither!" agreed Scooby, shaking his head. But after Velma negotiated with a sack of Scooby Snacks, Shaggy and Scooby agreed to help Mr. Samuels, too.

The kids packed for their trip. Fred, Velma, and Daphne brought life jackets, a rope, helmets, and a first-aid kit. Shaggy and Scooby brought lots of food—lots and lots of food!

"I'm afraid we can't fit all that food," said Daphne. "But don't worry, guys—we'll find lots of delicious nuts and berries to eat along the way," Velma told them.

"Groovy!" Shaggy rubbed his belly. "Like, I'm just nuts over nuts and berries!"

"Reah!" Scooby licked his lips. "Ruts and rerries!"

The gang set out, coasting down the beautiful blue river, enjoying the pleasant countryside and refreshing mountain air.

But soon things started going wrong. Shaggy and Scooby kept seeing something creepy in the bushes. It seemed to be following the gang's raft! Then, as the river began to flow faster, they saw that somebody . . . or something . . . had torn out the sign telling them which way they should go!

"Jinkies!" Velma exclaimed. "Without that sign, we could be headed right into the rapids and we wouldn't even know it!"

The gang had two choices in picking the right fork in the river to take. Unfortunately, they picked the wrong one! Soon the river was going from calm to choppy. Big boulders appeared in the water, and the gang had to steer around them as quickly as they could.

Then the river tumbled swiftly downhill, faster and faster! There were more and more rocks in the water. They were rafting through white-water rapids.

The kids valiantly struggled to stay afloat in the churning waters.

"Zoinks!" Shaggy cried. "I feel like I'm a milk shake that's about to be blended!"

"Roh, no!" Scooby hollered as he held on for dear life.

And though the rushing river was loud, they could hear laughter. Strange, creepy laughter!

When it looked as if they'd surely tumble into the dangerous water, Daphne spotted something up ahead.

"Over there! Try and steer that direction!" Daphne was pointing to a small stream that flowed off the main river.

They dug their oars into the water and steered with all their might. After a few nervous moments, they were floating swiftly down the small stream.

"Wow, that was close!" Fred wiped the sweat from his brow.

The kids were glad they'd gotten away from the rapids safely, but they still had the strange feeling they were being followed.

"We should make camp here for the night," Fred suggested. "I want to explore this area before it's too dark. I have a feeling that whatever happened to that sign was no accident."

The gang set up camp in a dry spot in the woods. As they worked, the fog got thicker and thicker. Everything was quiet and still — until they suddenly heard footsteps crunching through leaves.

"Jeepers! Who's that?" Daphne cried as a huge figure appeared through the mists.

"Zoinks!" Shaggy bellowed. "It's the m-m-marsh m-m-monster!"

"Ruh-roh!" Scooby jumped into Shaggy's arms and held on tight. But instead of a marsh monster, it was a man—a very large man.

"I may be as big as a bear, but I'm as friendly as a puppy!" he laughed. "They call me Big Dave, and I live in this forest."

The kids were all glad Big Dave wasn't the marsh monster. They invited him to join them for dinner. When they asked him if he'd seen the marsh monster, he said he hadn't. But he did talk about another kind of villain.

"Some people are trying to wreck this forest by using it for a toxic dumping ground," Big Dave told them sadly.

"Jinkies!" Velma frowned. "It would be terrible to ruin a beautiful forest like this!"

As everyone turned in for the night, they thought carefully about what Big Dave had told them.

In the morning, Big Dave said good-bye. He even gave them a going-away present — delicious nuts and berries from the forest!

"Thanks, Big Dave!" Velma waved. "After we've solved the marsh monster mystery, we'll do everything we can to save this forest."

After they'd drifted down the stream a couple miles, Fred spotted a clue—something big had broken tree branches near the edge of the water.

"It could be the marsh monster," Fred said as he steered the raft ashore. "C'mon, gang, let's investigate."

Shaggy and Scooby weren't too keen on getting out of the raft. When they finally did, they insisted on taking their sacks of food with them.

"Like, there's no way I'm gonna get grabbed by a greasy ghoul on an empty stomach," Shaggy declared firmly.

"Reah, ree reither!" Scooby agreed.

The kids crept carefully past the broken branches and into the forest. After they'd gone a few hundred feet, Fred stopped suddenly.

"Did you guys hear that?" he asked.

"Like, what?" Shaggy asked nervously.

All at once, a huge form jumped out from behind a tree. It was oily. It was slimy. It was the marsh monster!

"Rrrrroooowl!" it growled fiercely.

The Mystery, Inc., gang ran as fast as they could back toward the raft.

"Zoinks!" puffed Shaggy. "Now <u>that</u> I heard, but I wish I hadn't!"

The marsh monster was fast, but the gang was faster. Well, most of them were. Scooby and Shaggy couldn't bear to part with their food, even though they were in danger. Soon they were trapped!

As the marsh monster slowly approached them, Shaggy and Scooby looked at each other with dread.

"Like, Scoob, ol' pal . . . you know what we have to do," Shaggy cried.

Scooby was sobbing. "Rye row! Rye row!"

With that they both started throwing their food at the marsh monster.

The marsh monster didn't like getting pelted with food one bit. It backed off. When they saw their chance, Shaggy and Scooby ran for it.

When they got back to the others, Velma and Daphne started dressing Shaggy and Scooby in tree and bush branches.

"Just in time!" Fred smiled. "We've got a plan and we need you guys as bait."

After the girls were done, Scooby and Shaggy were fully camouflaged in leaves.

"Like, what a day!" Shaggy exclaimed. "First we lose our food, and now we might end up as ghoulie-grub!"

"Roulie-rub?" Scooby cried. "Roh, no!"

Shaggy and Scooby ventured back into the forest, looking for the marsh monster. Covered with branches and leaves, they were able to sneak right up next to it. Shaggy tapped the creature on the shoulder.

"Like, isn't this a mahh-velous costume party?" Shaggy grinned. "My pal and I came as matching foliage. But I see you went for the garbage disposal look."

"Rrrrrowl!"

The angry marsh monster was soon chasing them through the forest again. Scooby and Shaggy climbed into the trees to stay out of its slimy clutches.

"Hey, Scooby," Shaggy called as they climbed across branches, hopping from tree to tree. "Like, you're doing pretty good! I always thought dogs couldn't climb trees!"

"Rogs ran't rimb rees?" Scooby gulped. Then he promptly fell to the ground.

"Zoinks! Like, maybe I shouldn't have said that!" cried Shaggy. He dropped down to the ground with Scooby.

The two took off running. The marsh monster was gaining on them. They could hardly keep out of the fiend's oily grasp.

Scooby-Doo and Shaggy ran toward the river, heading right to the spot that Fred had told them about. They passed Daphne, hiding behind the trunk of a tree. She signaled to Velma and Fred.

The marsh monster reached its slimy hand toward Scooby and Shaggy. It was just inches from grabbing them.

"Now!" cried Fred. He and Velma leaned on an oar they'd wedged under a big boulder. Splash! The boulder hit the water. Suddenly, the fast-moving current of the river was diverted—right at the marsh monster.

Whooooosh! The powerful rush of water knocked the monster off its slimy feet!

Fred quickly tied up the marsh monster with a rope he'd brought from the raft. When he pulled at the creature's head, Mr. Peabody's assistant, Hank, was revealed. Hank dropped a walkie-talkie from under his costume.

"I wonder who he was communicating with," Daphne said as she picked it up.

"I think I know!" said Big Dave as he walked out of the woods. In one mighty fist he carried Mr. Peabody, who also had a walkie-talkie.

"Put me down, you lummox!" Mr. Peabody cried. "You can't do this to me!"

"Peabody had Hank pretend to be the marsh monster to scare away visitors. He hoped that would force Mr. Samuels to sell his rafting business," Velma said. "And it almost worked!"

255

With the mystery of the marsh monster solved, the gang was ready to return to their rafting trip. Shaggy and Scooby restocked the raft with plenty of food—including nuts and berries, of course.

"Kids, you saved my business!" Mr. Samuels waved as the gang started off down the river. "I can't thank you enough!"

"And you prevented a greedy man from ruining another precious forest!" called Big Dave.

"Like, it was our pleasure ... and our duty," said Shaggy with a grin. "Right, Scoob?"

"Scooby-Dooby-Doo," cheered Scooby.